r Books Weekly Reader Books Weekly Reader
er Books Weekly Reader Books Weekly Reader Books Weekly Rea
der Books Weekly Reader Books Weekly Reader Books Weekly R
eader Books Weekly Reader Books Weekly Reader Books Weekly
Reader Books Weekly Reader Books Weekly Reader Books Week
y Reader Books Weekly Reader Books Weekly Reader Books We
kly Reader Books Weekly Reader Books Weekly Reader Books W
eekly Reader Books Weekly Reader Books Weekly Reader Books
Weekly Reader Books Weekly Reader Books Weekly Reader Book
s Weekly Reader Books Weekly Reader Books Weekly Reader Bo
oks Weekly Reader Books Weekly Reader Books Weekly Reader B
Books Weekly Reader Books Weekly Reader Books Weekly Reade
er Books Weekly Reader Books Weekly Reader Books Weekly Rea
der Books Weekly Reader Books Weekly Reader Books Weekly Re
eader Books Weekly Reader Books Weekly Reader Books Weekly
Reader Books Weekly Reader Books Weekly Reader Books Week
y Reader Books Weekly Reader Books Weekly Reader Books Wee
kly Reader Books Weekly Reader Books Weekly Reader Books W

Weekly Reader Books Presents

A WORD TO THE WISE

Alison Cragin Herzig
Jane Lawrence Mali

Illustrated by Martha Perske

Boston Little, Brown and Company Toronto

For
Polly Washburn Cragin and Stuart Wilson Cragin
and for Kate and Adair

This book is a presentation of Weekly Reader Books. Weekly Reader Books offers book clubs for children from preschool through high school. For further information write to: **Weekly Reader Books,** 4343 Equity Drive, Columbus, Ohio 43228

Edited for Weekly Reader Books and published by arrangement with Little, Brown and Company. Weekly Reader is a federally registered trademark of Field Publications.

Third Printing

Library of Congress Cataloging in Publication Data

Herzig, Alison Cragin.
A word to the wise.

SUMMARY: The thesaurus stolen from their teacher alters the lives of eight fifth-graders in a special reading group.
[1. Vocabulary — Fiction. 2. School stories] I. Mali, Jane Lawrence, joint author. II. Perske, Martha. III. Title.
PZ7.H432478.Wo [Fic] 78-17447
ISBN 0-316-35898-3

Published simultaneously in Canada
by Little, Brown & Company (Canada) Limited
MV
Printed in the United States of America

1

"SHE'S TRYING TO poison us, said Willie. "Slowly. A few at a time. So we don't all drop dead at once. And there's never any ketchup."

He stood staring at the menu posted just inside the doors of the cafeteria. FRIDAY, OCTOBER 14TH was typed in capital letters across the top. The rest of O Group was nowhere in sight. Willie figured they were strung out along the stairs or still back in the classroom stashing their reading workbooks. All except for Henry. Henry was breathing down his neck. Willie couldn't stand it. Henry was fat and usually he lumbered along far behind everyone else—but not on his way to lunch. Somehow at lunch period he always managed to make it from the fourth floor to the basement as if he'd slid down a pole.

Beyond the serving area a second set of doors opened into the lunchroom. The din and clatter stampeded

Willie, but he was already flattened by the smell of the food. It made his throat close up and his stomach lurch. Breathing through his mouth helped, but he still had to look at the mustard-yellow walls that were even darker yellow in the corners and near the ceiling. One of the fluorescent lights above his head flickered dimly.

"Oh good," said Henry, "there's hardly any line."

"No wonder," Willie said. "It's codfish cakes and succotash again. The other kids probably died from the smell."

"Who died, Willie?" It was Grace. Willie groaned through clenched teeth. Grace had decided she liked him at the beginning of the year and now she followed him everywhere. There she was, right behind Henry, her dumb ponytails sticking out behind each ear and her bangs so long they got tangled up in her eyelashes. Willie wished her bangs would grow all the way to her chin; then she wouldn't be able to see and he could ditch her—easy.

"Who did you say died?"

"Nobody—yet," Willie told her.

There was a crash from the lunchroom followed by applause and shrieks of laughter. If all three hundred kids were still in there, figured Willie, the gym would be empty. He pictured himself all alone dribbling and dodging across the vast polished floor. I could cut lunch, he thought, and duck upstairs. Henry can have seconds on fish cakes.

"What's for dessert?" asked Henry.

"Jell-O. It's always Jell-O," said Willie. He looked at the menu again. "No! Hang on—Jell-O and ice-cream sandwiches."

"Ice-cream sandwiches? Really?" asked Grace.

"Ice . . . cream . . . sandwiches." Henry inhaled each word. Then he held his breath and swallowed as if the words were the real thing. Willie turned to look at him. If Henry were a slot machine his eyes would be dinging up ice-cream sandwiches for sure. Under the right circumstances, Henry might even kill for food, Willie thought. He would certainly eat anything. Once, after Henry had been over to his house for the afternoon, Willie had found teeth marks in the wax apple in the bowl on the kitchen table.

Grace handed Willie a tray. I guess it's worth it, he thought, for the dessert. "Hold your nose, Henry, till we're past the succotash," Willie advised. As they neared the pile of vegetables, Henry only pretended to hold his nose; Willie knew he was happily sniffing.

One behind the other, they slid their trays along the stainless-steel bars of the serving counter. There she was, getting closer and closer: Mrs. Cleft, the dietician, towering over her steaming pans, waving her iron ladle.

"Can you see the desserts?" asked Henry.

"There are still a lot left," said Willie, standing on tiptoes. Craning his neck to see over taller kids, he tried to keep the ice-cream sandwiches in sight.

"How many?" asked Henry.

"Two, four . . ." A group of teachers butted into line ahead of them. The dessert counter was blocked from view.

"Only four?"

Willie didn't answer. He was suddenly tired of Henry and tired of Grace and tired of standing on tiptoes to see over people.

Just ahead of them, Mrs. Cleft ladled away. Sweat beaded her upper lip and her hairnet was coming unpinned. *Glop, splat; glop, splat*—first the succotash, then the fish cakes.

Grace shook her head and blew her bangs out of her eyes. "Mrs. Cleft, the bottoms of my fish cakes are *green*!" she wailed.

"Greens are good for you," said Mrs. Cleft. "Move along now." But there was nothing to move along to. When they reached the dessert counter, all the ice-cream sandwiches were gone.

The three of them stood for a moment staring at the rows of Jell-O. "Might as well," muttered Henry finally. "Shouldn't let them go to waste."

"We're always too late," said Grace, looking balefully at the crowded tables nearest to her. "Fifth grade stinks."

"It's O Group that stinks," said Willie. "E Group gets to go to lunch early."

"Bet they took seconds," said Henry. "Maybe they couldn't finish them." There were two large garbage cans lined with plastic bags just beyond the doorway into the lunchroom. He balanced his tray on the edge of one of them and bent over the can to check its contents. Willie watched, fascinated, as Henry's tray tilted and his plate began to slide. I should warn him, he thought—but it was too late. Henry's lunch picked up speed and tumbled into the trash.

"Oh, no!" gasped Henry. He grabbed for the Jell-O, but missed.

"Oh, yes," said Willie.

Henry stared at his empty tray.

"Good shot! Best place for it anyway," said Willie. He dumped his own lunch on top of Henry's and stuffed the tray in after it. He didn't care who saw him do it.

"Willie, you're not supposed to do that!" said Grace. "You're supposed to stack your tray by the door. Mrs. Cleft has a you-know-what if you don't stack."

"I would have eaten yours," said Henry sadly.

"Go ahead," said Willie in disgust. "I've had it." He turned and started for the door.

"Wait up, Willie. So long, Henry," said Grace. "Where're you going, Willie?"

"To the gym," Willie told her without looking back. He could hear her footsteps behind him.

"I'll come with you," said Grace. "I dumped my lunch, too."

Figures, thought Willie.

Willie wanted to work on his lay-ups, but Grace's dribbling and dropshots kept throwing him off. She made one lucky basket after another and once, when their shots collided in midair, hers went in and his didn't. Willie glanced at the gym clock and cut his practice session short, but even so, when he reached the library, with Grace jogging at his heels, he could see through the windowed doors that most of O Group was already there. I could have made it on time if the library weren't on the top floor, thought Willie sourly. The whole school is against me. The sight of O Group proved it. The library was as big and awesome as the gym. It felt like a museum to Willie, with its hundreds of books lining the walls, ordered and numbered, and the heavy, dark reading tables with their shaded lamps. It looked so important and grown-up, all of it—except for the table O Group had to use. That table was over by the windows in the bright sunlight, away from the big shelves. It was low and light-colored and the chairs around it were light-colored too, with sawed-off legs and no arms. O Group looked silly and stupid sitting there. Mrs. Dillworth, the special-reading teacher, looked almost as dumb. She had to sit at a rickety card table stacked with books and papers, but at least she was closer to the big shelves and the sun didn't get in her eyes.

"You're late," said Mrs. Dillworth. "The bell rang some time ago. The boat has already left the dock, so to speak. Who else is missing?"

"I am—or I was," said Fuzzle. He tripped over the doorsill coming in.

"Tie your shoelaces, dear," Mrs. Dillworth told him, "and sit down, the three of you. Time and tide wait for no person." She smiled at Grace.

Willie pulled out the chair next to Henry. Books were scattered all over the table. Most of them were thin and some had big lettering and bright pictures on the covers. Willie had the feeling he was being pushed backward in time. Any day now he would find himself in the first grade cutting out pictures of things that began with the letter *A*. Looking across the table at Beegee didn't help. Beegee was the shortest boy in the fifth grade and was probably shorter than all the boys in the fourth and third grades, too. He was so short that he had to stand on his toes to use the drinking fountains.

"Mrs. Cleft's gone nuts," Henry whispered. "She's been through the garbage cans twice."

"How do you know?" asked Willie.

"I went back for seconds—firsts, really. No point starving to death."

Fuzzle was feeling under the table, trying to tie his shoelaces without looking.

"Now then, we can get started," said Mrs. Dillworth, standing up. She came and hung over their table, supporting herself on her knuckles. Somehow she reminded Willie of a beach umbrella.

"I'm right in the middle of making new blend cards," she said, "for those tricky *th* and *ch* words, so today you'll have to work on your own. I think that will be fun, don't you?" She sounded as if she were asking them if they liked Halloween. "I want you to read silently to yourselves, but watch out for punctuation and phrasing. Thelma, why don't you play that four-syllable word game we started last time. You would benefit from that too, Amanda."

"Oh, that was such fun!" said Amanda, lifting her

long hair off her neck with both hands and then letting it fall down her back. It was light brown and curled slightly at the ends. Willie noticed she was wearing one of those shirts of hers imported from Paris, France. He could tell because it was printed all over with *C*'s.

Thelma stared at Mrs. Dillworth without blinking. She didn't say anything.

"And Francis," said Mrs. Dillworth. Fuzzle stopped trying to find his shoelaces and looked up. His chin rested on the table. "Pay very close attention to the *where, what,* and *when* words."

"What?" asked Fuzzle. Mrs. Dillworth didn't hear him.

"And remember to use your pencils and notebooks." Willie knew by the startled expression on Fuzzle's face that he'd just remembered that he'd forgotten his. Even though his hair and his eyes were almost black, Fuzzle usually looked foggy, as if he'd just woken up, thought Willie. "Jot down any words that you don't understand," Mrs. Dillworth went on. "All right, then. Shoulders to the wheel, now. But silently, please. I've got other fish to fry." Mrs. Dillworth straightened up and turned away from the table.

"Lots of times I don't know what she means," whispered Beegee. "Sounds like she's going to make more lunch."

"Some of my father's friends talk like that," said Jonathan, taking a pencil from the pocket of his shirt. His notebook was already open. Sunlight glinted off the metal frames of his glasses. The earpieces ended in big hooks that curved all the way around behind Jonathan's ears and up a little in front of his earlobes.

"Anyone see a book on horses?" asked Amanda.

"Here's one about a circus," said Grace. "That do?"

Amanda looked at the bright yellow cover. "I've

read it, a million times," she said. "I've memorized it. I can read it with my eyes closed."

"Why don't you ask Dillworth for something else?" Willie suggested.

"She already did," Thelma told him. Thelma was cool, thought Willie. She wore beat-up track shoes and crazy T-shirts and she was even taller than he was. Willie wouldn't have minded if Thelma instead of Grace had latched on to him.

"What did she say?" he asked.

Thelma pinched up her mouth and crossed her eyes. "I have put a broad selection of lovely books on your table, suitable for your reading level."

"Figures," said Willie.

"Rockets—there's nothing here about rockets," mumbled Fuzzle. Henry's stomach rumbled and gurgled. He sounded as if he might erupt any minute.

"There's nothing here about anything," said Willie, "unless you're into monkeys or mice. How did I get stuck with these jerks, these creeps, these nurds? thought Willie. "I'm going to the big shelves." Mrs. Dillworth was bent over her blend cards. Willie got up quickly and slipped across the room. So far, so good.

"What do you think you're doing, young man?"

Willie stood motionless, facing the rows of books. "Looking for something to read," he said.

"You know perfectly well you're not allowed to use the big shelves," said Mrs. Dillworth sternly.

"E Group does."

"O Group isn't ready yet.

"What am I going to read then?"

"Anything on your table. I've told you that a dozen times before. Back you go now. The period's half over."

Jonathan pulled out Willie's chair for him. "You tried," he said, "and that's what counts."

"No, it isn't." Willie started to say something about the importance of winning but then he remembered about Jonathan's father and stopped.

"I really should be in E Group," said Amanda wistfully. "My governess says I read beautifully and with great expression."

"I wonder if you can get out of O Group once you are in it, or is it for life?" said Beegee.

"I'm gonna get out," said Thelma. "Just wait."

"Ditto," said Willie.

Five weeks before, their homeroom teacher had divided the class into the E's and the O's, for reading.

"These are just letters," he had said. "They don't stand for anything special. Elephants and orangutans, eggplants and oranges—just letters."

"Who does he think he's kidding? That old trick has never fooled me," Willie had said when the teacher went next door to borrow some chalk. E Group had gone to lunch; O Group was working on their reading skills.

"Take a look at who's here," Willie went on. "Henry-O, Thelma-O, Jonathan-O, Grace-O, Fuzzle-O, Beegee-O, Amanda-O, and Me-O."

"Ho, ho," said Thelma. "The zee-rOs."

"The dummies," said Fuzzle sadly.

"EEEither you're a good reader, OOOr you're not," said Beegee.

Mrs. Dillworth had decided they weren't and had told their homeroom teacher. Which was why they were now sitting at a special table in the library listening to Henry's stomach rumble.

"Rockets, rockets . . ." Fuzzle was still pawing through the books in front of him. "What's this?" He uncovered a book with only writing on the cover that was much fatter and heavier than the others. "Maybe," said Fuzzle, squinting at the title. "Maybe not." He opened it anyway.

"What have you got?" asked Amanda. "Something on horses?"

"Naw," said Fuzzle, pushing it away. "It's just a book full of words."

"Good heavens!" said Mrs. Dillworth as she came over to check on their progress. "What is that doing here?" She reached for the book.

Willie reached for it at the same time. "Fuzzle's reading it," he said.

"I am?"

"Don't be ridiculous. Francis can't read that book."

"Yes he can. He did. Didn't you, Fuzzle?" Willie gave Fuzzle a kick under the table.

"Um, yeah," said Fuzzle, "but it's just a dumb book full of words."

"That is precisely my point," said Mrs. Dillworth. "He—you—are not ready. You can't yet recognize a gold mine when you see one."

"A gold mine?" said Willie, getting a better grip on his end of the book.

"A gem of the first water. A treasure—an absolute treasure." Mrs. Dillworth pulled the book toward her.

"A treasure?" Willie hung on.

"Let go, dear," said Mrs. Dillworth. "It's the only copy in the library and the older classes need it."

"I'm reading it," said Willie.

"Someday I hope you will be," said Mrs. Dillworth. "Then there will be no stopping you. But for now it's going back on the big shelf."

She yanked. Willie held on, and he and the book slid halfway across the table.

"I want to read it," panted Willie. "It was on the table."

"Please, Mrs. Dillworth. You said we could read anything on the table," Amanda reminded her.

"But this shouldn't have been on the table in the first place," said Mrs. Dillworth.

"But it was," said Jonathan.

"It *is!*" said Willie, holding it down with all his strength.

"And you said . . ." Thelma insisted.

Mrs. Dillworth let go. Willie fell back into his chair with the book clutched to his chest.

"All right, Willie," said Mrs. Dillworth coldly. "We won't make an issue of it, will we? Since you insist, you may have the book this once—for this period only. Is that clear? But remember, treat it with the respect it deserves."

"Big deal," said Thelma when Mrs. Dillworth had retreated. "The period's practically over."

"Let me see it." Grace reached across the table.

"I'm after you," said Jonathan.

"Me next," said Beegee.

"Wait a sec," said Willie.

"We haven't got a sec," said Thelma. "The bell's about to ring."

Willie looked up at the clock.

"You're right. We've got four lousy minutes."

"Maybe if we ask Mrs. Dillworth very politely she'll let us sign it out for today," suggested Amanda.

"Fat chance," said Henry. "She said just this period."

"Chalk one up for Mrs. Dillworth," said Beegee, licking his finger and making a stroke in the air.

"Not yet," said Willie. "There must be something we can do."

Willie had never wanted to read anything before except biographies of basketball players—but this book was different. It was thick and heavy and it suddenly seemed like the only worthwhile book that had ever been on their table. Willie was sick of being told what he could read and what he couldn't read.

He was sick of being picked on. He didn't even know what this book was about, but he was determined to find out. He wanted the book more than Henry wanted ice-cream sandwiches.

"I know," he said. "We'll steal it."

2

"STEALING'S FINE BY me," said Thelma.

"Me too," said Grace.

The others stared at Willie in silence, except for Amanda. Amanda looked horrified.

"Stealing is bad," she sputtered. "Like shoplifting. It's not nice—and besides, we might get caught!"

"If we were starving and we stole some food because no one would give us any, would that be wrong too?" asked Willie.

"Definitely not," said Henry. "I say take it."

"But with food you never have to go back to that same market again. You can have it delivered or shop somewhere else," said Amanda. "But we have to face Mrs. Dillworth every Friday."

"I've never stolen anything before," said Jonathan.

"This isn't just anything," Amanda told him. "It's a big thing. And it's the only copy. Mrs. Dillworth said so. She'll catch us for sure."

"She finds things out just by staring at you," agreed Jonathan.

"And she adores books," whispered Amanda, leaning forward. "She gets simply furious if you crack the spine or get one the teeniest bit wet. Remember what she did when I dropped that book in the bathtub by mistake?" Amanda shuddered.

"She ripped up a note from my mother once, right in front of my face," said Grace.

"And she hounds you and hounds you until you could die of embarrassment if your book's only a day overdue," Amanda added. "Think what she'd do if we stole one!"

"She's fierce all right," said Jonathan. "I even know some seventh-graders who are scared of her."

"Sometimes she can be nice," said Beegee. "The problem is, you never know when."

"Why don't we steal a book on rockets, instead?" suggested Fuzzle.

"Why call it stealing?" asked Thelma. "We're just taking it without signing for it. We can always return it, ya know."

"Not like food," said Henry. "Once you've eaten it, it's gone."

"I don't care what you call it and I'm not scared of Dillworth," said Willie, "but we've got to decide—and fast. Let's vote. All in favor, raise a finger."

Amanda put her hands in her lap and looked around. She saw Jonathan's finger bend and then straighten. Everyone else already had a finger in the air. Willie was watching her. Amanda raised a hand to examine her nails and check her watch and her rings and the wart on the tip of her thumb.

"Okay. It's unanimous. We take it," Willie said.

"How?" asked Fuzzle.

"Easy." Thelma reached for the book. She weighed

it in her hands. "It's heavier than I thought. Never mind—I can do it. But I'll need some help."

"I'll help," offered Willie.

"Okay. Distract Dillworth. Knock over your chair. Make a lot of noise. Anything, but keep the heat off me. I'll do the rest."

"There's the bell," announced Willie.

He pushed a pile of books off the table. A chair crashed to the floor. Henry crashed to the floor.

"Look out," warned Beegee, "here comes Dillworth."

Mrs. Dillworth circled her card table and advanced upon them.

Thelma rose and headed toward the door, ignoring the uproar. She walked right by Mrs. Dillworth, looking straight ahead and taking small, dignified steps.

"What's going on here?" demanded Mrs. Dillworth when she reached the table. "What have you done to those books?"

"Nothing," said Willie. "Just cleaning up." He righted a chair. Grace and Fuzzle picked the last of the books off the floor.

"Good-bye, Mrs. Dillworth," said Amanda. "I'm sorry for everything."

"Well, I must say, it wasn't precisely the silent reading practice I had in mind," allowed Mrs. Dillworth, "but sometimes one aims at a pigeon and kills a crow. I think we'll go back to Lotto next time."

Amanda hurried out of the library after the others. Thelma was waiting for them by the stairs at the end of the hall.

"Now what?" she said when they reached her.

"Where's the book?" Fuzzle peered at her. Thelma's hands were empty.

"Between my knees, stupid," Thelma told him. "But I can't squeeze forever. It's slipping!"

They heard footsteps pounding on the stairs.

"Quick," said Willie. He opened the nearest door. "In here."

"Oh, gross!" said Amanda. "A cleaning closet. Wild horses couldn't drag me in there."

"In," said Willie, "and shut up."

Amanda went, propelled by Grace. When Thelma had pigeon-toed past him followed by the others, Willie closed the door.

"Where's the light?"

"I can't see."

"Neither can I."

"Turn on the light."

"I'm trying to find it."

There was a crash and a clanging.

"Geez. I think I'm stuck in something."

"Somebody get the light."

"Oh, gag! There are slimies everywhere."

"I think I found it."

The light went on.

If the closet had been empty, there would have been room to spare—but it wasn't. Beegee was wedged between deep double sinks and a stack of cardboard cartons labeled TOILET TISSUE. Henry stood with one foot in a bucket and Grace was swatting wet mop strands out of her face.

Gray rags hung from a makeshift clothesline, and brooms, mops, vacuum cleaners, and floor waxers leaned against the walls. The floor was littered with metal buckets and plastic bottles full of green liquid.

"Oh, gross!" said Amanda again.

"This is a cleaning closet?" asked Grace. "It smells worse than the lunchroom."

"Cut the complaining," said Willie. "We haven't got all day. We're only supposed to take five minutes between classes, ya know. Let's see it, Thelma."

Thelma reached under her skirt.

"Lucky I wasn't wearing blue jeans." She held the book up and waved it back and forth. The others looked at her with admiration. Grace reached for the book.

"Sit down, everyone," said Willie.

"Where? How?" asked Fuzzle.

"On a bucket, stupid," said Willie. "But keep it quiet."

They turned some of the buckets bottom end up. Grace and Jonathan shared one; and Amanda, before sitting down, wiped hers off with a rag from the clothesline. Beegee squatted in one of the sinks and Willie knelt on the floor. He glanced up at Henry, who remained standing near the door.

Henry shrugged his shoulders and looked at his feet. Oh geez, thought Willie, typical—he's got his foot stuck in that bucket. Willie pretended he hadn't noticed.

"Give me the book, Thelma," said Willie.

Clang, clank, crash! Beegee and Fuzzle giggled.

"Henry, shut up. Keep your foot quiet." Sometimes Henry seemed to be klutzy on purpose, thought Willie.

"Okay, Thelma," said Willie, "let's see the book."

Thelma ignored him. "It's called *The Students' Thesore-us.*"

"Oh," said Fuzzle, "dinosaurs, maybe."

"No like you said in the library, words." Thelma continued to read the cover. "It says '*Two hundred and forty thousand words and phrases.*'"

"I didn't know there were that many words in the whole world," said Beegee.

"Neither did I," said Amanda.

"Nobody knows that many words—not even my father," said Jonathan, "and he gives speeches all the time."

"Somebody must,"said Thelma. "Somebody wrote it."

"How many words did you say, Thelma?" asked Fuzzle.

"Two hundred and forty thousand," Thelma repeated, and then added, "*'The right word at the right time.'*"

"Who cares," said Beegee. "I don't even know why we stole it."

"Yeah, Willie." Fuzzle looked puzzled. "Why did we steal it, anyway? Huh, Willie?"

At the mention of his name everyone in the cleaning closet looked at him. Willie stood up and folded his arms across his chest. Slowly, he put his hands into his pockets. First one, then the other. All the time he was thinking, thinking.

"Because . . ." he drew the word out. He glanced at the thesaurus. If ever he needed the right word, it was now.

"Because, it's a gold mine, remember?" he continued. "Besides, it's too late to take it back now."

"Willie's right," said Grace. "We're stuck with it."

Willie sat down again. At least Grace was on his side. Better Grace than no one.

"But it's Mrs. Dillworth's only copy. She's probably looking for it right now. We're going to get into a lot of trouble," moaned Amanda.

"Not unless somebody squeals," said Thelma.

"And nobody's going to. Because"—Willie slitted his eyes—"we're going to swear an oath of secrecy. A blood oath." He pulled a jackknife out of his pocket.

"You're not allowed to bring weapons to school," said Amanda.

"Oh, come off it, Amanda," said Thelma. "You'd scream about a water pistol."

“I don’t mind somebody else’s blood,” said Beegee, “but my blood makes me sick.”

“You first, Willie,” said Jonathan firmly.

“I’ll go last,” said Grace.

“Gangrene,” said Amanda. “I think you get gangrene from germy knives.”

“Okay, okay.” Willie decided not to press it. Besides, the big blade was hard to get out, the little blade was broken, and the bottle opener didn’t seem right for a blood oath. “We’ll just swear,” he said.

"I know an oath," said Jonathan. "Everyone raise your right hand. You too, Henry."

Willie looked at Henry. Holding the bucket with both hands, Henry was bent over wiggling his stuck foot and grunting softly. Poor old Hen, thought Willie—even his foot's too fat.

"Henry," he said sharply, "we're swearing."

Henry straightened and raised his hand slowly. "I swear to tell the truth, the whole truth, and nothing but the truth, so help me God," intoned Jonathan.

"That's crazy." Thelma lowered her arm. "If we tell the truth—" She stopped abruptly and ran her finger across her throat.

"I know!" said Grace. "If you tell, you stink, you smell, and, and—and you'll go to hell"—she looked at Willie—"and fry and yell. How's that?"

"Okay, okay," said Willie.

"So now what do we do with this gold mine—if it really is one, which I doubt?" asked Amanda after they had sworn.

"Yeah, what do we do now?" asked Fuzzle.

"The next period's practically started, and I hate being late," said Amanda.

"We read it," said Willie. "Mrs. Dillworth said once you've read it, there's no stopping you."

"All of it?" wailed Amanda.

"Maybe not all of it," said Willie, eyeing the book, "but parts of it. We'll take turns. Who wants to go first?"

Nobody spoke.

"You, Thelma?"

"I already went first. I stole it."

Willie could feel Grace, sitting beside him, just itching to be asked. He turned away and looked at Henry instead. Henry was bent over again, this time fiddling with his shoelaces. Knowing Henry, they're double-knotted, Willie thought.

"Okay," Willie said, "Beegee gets it."

Beegee peered over the edge of the sink. He watched the book come toward him, passed from hand to hand.

"Why me?" he asked.

"Somebody has to. I thought maybe you'd like being first." Willie searched for another reason. "You're a pretty good speller, you know."

Beegee accepted the book reluctantly and held it out in front of him.

"What am I supposed to do with it?" he asked, worry lines wrinkling his forehead.

"Find out why it's so super and report back to me," said Willie.

"Report? Where? When?" asked Fuzzle.

"Monday. Same time, same place," said Willie.

"We can't do it same time. Monday afternoon we have posture pictures," Jonathan reminded him.

"At recess, then. Same place."

"In this yucky cleaning closet?" said Amanda.

"Same place," said Willie firmly. "It's safe. Nobody looks in here."

"They'll be looking everywhere if we don't get moving," said Thelma.

"I can't just walk around holding this book," said Beegee.

"Wrap it in this rag," said Amanda, handing him a gray square from the clothesline.

"Okay?" said Willie. "Everybody ready?"

"No," said Henry. "My foot—it's still in the bucket."

So Jonathan held the bucket down, and Willie managed to free Henry's foot.

"Oh boy, thanks," said Henry. "Thanks a lot."

"Okay," asked Willie again, "everybody ready?"

"Yeah, thanks to you," said Henry.

Willie opened the door a crack.

"Ready, Beegee? Coast is clear. Act natural."

"I was afraid I'd have to wear it home," said Henry. "Gee, Willie, thanks!"

Willie wanted to slam a bucket over Henry's head, but he didn't.

"Everybody out," he said.

3

BEEGEE COULD SEE Mr. Metzger from two blocks away, sunning himself on a folding canvas stool. On good days, he was always there, just to the right of the door, "taking the air." At the red light, Beegee stopped and waited, his book bag dragging at his shoulder. Through the thin canvas, he could feel the edge of the thesaurus bumping against his knee. This bag must weigh sixty pounds, he thought, and then he remembered that he himself didn't weigh that much, even with all his clothes on. Forty pounds then, at least.

From one block away Beegee saw Mr. Metzger moving his head from side to side, watching the people walk by in front of him. The old man wore a hat with the brim up, all the way around. That's the way he liked it. Around the turned-up collar of his blue coat, he'd wound his maroon muffler, several times. Mr.

Metzger always wore the hat, the coat, and the muffler no matter what the weather and he always looked cold. Beegee decided it must be his skin: it was so thin. It was like tracing paper; everything showed underneath it. Now that Beegee was used to them, he didn't mind the lines and little red squiggles in Mr. Metzger's face and the brown blotches on the backs of his hands.

Mr. Metzger was the oldest person Beegee knew, a great-grandfather at least. Everything about him was old: his eyes, his ears, his books, his couch—everything.

"Well, Friend Beegee. A good afternoon."

"Hi, Mr. Metzger."

"Did you bring the pumpkin seeds?"

"Yes," answered Beegee. "I have them in my book bag."

"Splendid. Let's go upstairs. I've taken enough air to fill all the dusty crevices in my attic." Mr. Metzger tapped his head and looked at Beegee knowingly. "Where's my cane?"

Beegee knew it was better if he didn't try to help him get up, but he stood close by just in case. Mr. Metzger took a deep breath and tilted forward in slow motion until he was off his stool. Once on his feet and moving, he didn't stop, but made straight for the door, taking very small steps.

"You left your stool, Mr. Metzger," Beegee called after him. "I'll get it."

The lobby hall was long and mirrored. Beegee balanced on one foot and then on the other, taking slow, slow steps, trying to keep his pace down to match Mr. Metzger's shuffle. We're almost the same size, thought Beegee, as he watched their reflection in the mirror. It was a little hard to tell because Mr. Metzger sort of curved over at the top, like a question mark.

As soon as they heard the apartment door open,

the parakeets went into their act. They hopped back and forth on their perches, swung, and raced up ladders, their claws clicking on the plastic bars. All the time, they bobbed their heads and murmured deep in their throats. Beegee still had trouble telling them apart. He'd learned which were boys and which were girls by the band of color above their beaks. Blue for boys, brown for girls, Mr. Metzger said. But Florence Nightingale looked just like Cleopatra, and Teddy Roosevelt, Churchill, and Babe Ruth flew around in a blur of blue and green and purple. He'd finally figured out that Florence called herself Cleo and that Teddy Roosevelt liked to hang upside down, and that had helped.

The old man stuck his cane in the umbrella stand just inside the front door and moved toward the kitchen.

"What are we drinking today? Milk? Root beer? Formosa oolong?" He paused at the kitchen door.

"Formosa oolong," said Beegee.

Mr. Metzger nodded and disappeared around the corner. Beegee remembered the time when he thought all tea came in little bags. Oolong came loose in a can and was served in cups without handles.

Beegee shrugged off his book bag and let it thump to the hallway floor. He was relieved to be rid of it until he remembered the thesaurus. It was still there, taking up a lot of space. Beegee had to feel around it for the bag of pumpkin seeds.

In the kitchen, he found Mr. Metzger standing at the counter pouring milk into two glasses. Beegee didn't mind that he'd forgotten. Milk's better when you're thirsty, he thought.

"Mr. Metzger? Have you ever stolen anything?"

Mr. Metzger stopped pouring and put the carton down.

"Certainly."

"Like what?"

"I'm going to sit down. Might help me remember."

"I'll bring the milks," said Beegee, picking up the glasses. "You go first."

The parakeets were still clicking and clacking and twimmering. They sound like a bunch of little typewriters, thought Beegee. He put the milk and the seeds on the table, next to Mr. Metzger's chair.

Mr. Metzger lowered himself carefully. He was still in his coat, scarf, and hat.

"Want me to take your hat?" asked Beegee.

"No, thank you." Mr. Metzger put it on top of the lampshade.

"About the stealing," prompted Beegee. "Have you remembered?"

"Yes," said Mr. Metzger. "Once I stole a chicken. And apples, lots of apples, of course; and much paraphernalia from hotels—ashtrays and bath mats, that sort of thing. What did you steal?"

"I'm not sure," said Beegee. "Want to see it?"

"Indeed I do!"

Beegee ran to get the thesaurus. When he returned he found that Mr. Metzger had dozed off, but he woke with a start when Beegee put the book in his lap. First he looked at it through his glasses. Then he pulled his glasses down to the end of his nose and tried peering over them. Finally, raising the book close to his face, he tilted his head back and, through his glasses again, inspected the cover.

"What's this?"

"What I stole."

"A thesaurus? You stole a thesaurus?"

"Well, not just me. My whole group."

"Astounding!" said Mr. Metzger. He opened the cover and began to turn the pages. "Remarkable group, yours. Astonishing, really." He sounded very pleased.

"Actually, I'm in the slow group, you know," said Beegee, "and Mrs. Dillworth says this book is too hard for us."

"Never met her," said Mr. Metzger, "but anyone who would think of stealing a thesaurus is pretty smart, if you ask me."

"You mean it? Can you show me how to use it?" asked Beegee.

"Of course." Mr. Metzger pulled out a glasses case, took out the wire spectacles that were in it, and replaced them with the ones he had been wearing on the end of his nose. His handkerchief ready, he fogged the new pair with his breath, polished them, held them up to the light, and polished some more. Finally he was ready. He cleared his throat.

"Alphabetized you see, like a dictionary." He tried to flip from back to front.

Beegee had a quick glance at some *Z* words first and then some *B* words. He thought he spied some *M*'s in the middle, but the pages went by too fast and in big clumps.

"Pick a word, my boy." Mr. Metzger was wide awake now.

"Uh, *book?*" suggested Beegee.

"Another word. Something with oomph."

"What about *steal*?" Beegee asked.

"*Steal.* Hmm. Yes. Good thinking." Mr. Metzger settled his shoulders into the back cushion. He crossed one leg over the other and opened the book.

"S, S, S-T, S-T-E . . ." he muttered, his eyes slowly following the column of words, first down and then back up the page. "Oh, drat it. I never can remember whether *L* comes before *K* or after it."

"Want me to find it? I'm a pretty good speller." Even Willie thought so.

"Good lad. I was hoping you were. Here."

"Okay," said Beegee after a moment. "I found *steal.* But there's a ton of words after it."

"Quite right," said Mr. Metzger cheerfully, "and they all mean 'steal' in one way or another. Read some."

Beegee hesitated. "There are a few that I can't pronounce," he said.

"Skip over them—just pick and choose the ones you like."

Beegee began to read aloud: "'*Rob, swipe, snitch, snatch, purloin, filch . . .*' "

"*Purloin.*" Mr. Metzger made a steeple with his fingers. "*Purloin*'s one of my favorites. I always like the ones that begin with *P—plunder, pilfer, pirate, poach, plagiarize.* Do you see *plagiarize* anywhere?"

"Yeah. I think so," said Beegee. "Yeah, right here. And after that there's *abduct* and *kidnap.*"

"Stop," said Mr. Metzger. He laughed like paper crackling. "You've gone too far. Now you're into stealing people."

Beegee pictured himself carrying Mrs. Dillworth, bound and gagged, from the library and stashing her in the cleaning closet. He laughed too. Mr. Metzger wheezed and wiped his eyes.

"Press on," he said. "Find another word."

Beegee turned one page and then two more.

"Here's an easy one. I use it all the time."

"Splendid! An overused word," said Mr. Metzger. "That's the kind of word a thesaurus is best for. Which one is it?"

Beegee put the book on Mr. Metzger's knee and hung over his shoulder. The old man adjusted his glasses. They read together until Mr. Metzger fell asleep in his chair.

Early Monday morning Beegee found the corridor

outside his classroom in an uproar. The gang of sixth-graders was at it again. Having managed to discover and memorize the combinations of most of the lockers on the floor, they were now zipping up and down twirling dials and opening doors. Just to prove how great they were. Metal clanged on metal. Doors swung on their hinges like shutters in the wind. The sixth-graders ordered younger kids to move aside and threatened to punch them if they didn't move fast enough.

Thelma was swearing a blue streak. She slammed her door shut again as soon as it was opened, in hopes of catching one of the gang by surprise and slicing off a few prying fingers. She just missed. Amanda had her hands over her ears. Only Fuzzle was happy. His combination lock was stiff and he was now examining the inside of his locker for the first time in days.

Bullies, thought Beegee. Not my locker, you won't. But how was he going to stop them? The mob banged and crashed their way toward him.

"Move over, Beegee."

"We're checking lockers."

"We want to look at your dial."

"See if it has enough numbers."

"Yeah."

Beegee straddled his book bag and faced them. The handle on his locker door pressed into his back.

"I'll open it myself," he said.

"That's what you think. Move over, stupid."

Stupid, thought Beegee, remembering. The thesaurus had really liked that word. He and Mr. Metzger had spent a lot of time making up crazy sentences. Beegee clenched his hands at his sides and took a deep breath.

"Bug off, nincompoops!" he shouted. "Fat-headed dizzards, driveling boobies!"

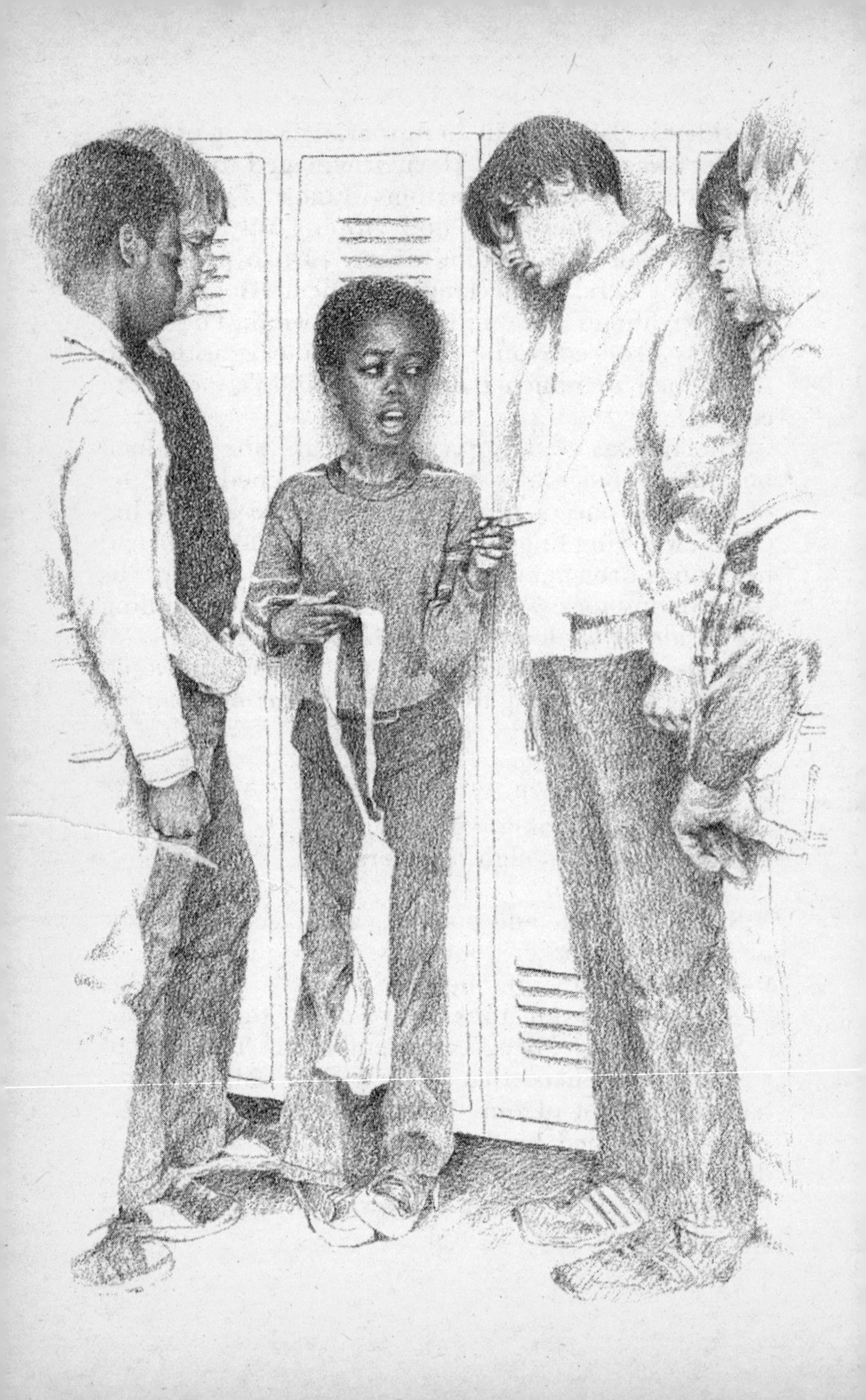

The sixth-graders stared at him. Beegee felt his ears get hot. He pictured the page in his mind.

"Noddies!" he yelled. "Nitwits, beetleheads, gowks!" The words spilled out. The hallway grew silent.

Beegee leaned forward and spoke loudly and clearly, drawing out each syllable: "Dun-der-pates!"

The sixth-graders hesitated, shuffling their feet and eyeing each other. They watched him warily.

Where is Willie? Beegee wondered. Willie wasn't scared of anything. His locker was the next one down, but Beegee didn't dare turn his head. The skin on the back of his neck prickled. Then he felt someone move in beside him.

"You heard what he said!" a voice shouted. It was Willie. Their shoulders were touching.

The sixth-graders didn't seem to know what to do. They were still standing there, undecided, when the bell rang.

"We'll get him tomorrow," said one of them to the others. He didn't sound too sure.

Beegee let out his breath silently. "No you won't." He stayed right where he was without moving until the gang of sixth-graders had backed off and started down the hall toward their classroom.

At recess, Beegee entered the cleaning closet carrying an oblong package wrapped in a page from the sports section of the Sunday newspaper. The others were already there. They had saved him the best bucket.

"Hey, Beeg," said Willie, "not bad. Those sixth-graders didn't have a clue."

"Me neither," said Thelma.

"'Driveling boobies,'" said Grace. "I liked that."

"'Dizzard' sounded sorta good." Henry licked his lips.

"But what do they mean?" asked Amanda.

"Good question," said Thelma.

"Stupid!" said Beegee.

"See this fist?" Thelma waved it in his face. "It's going right up your nose.

"Not you—the words. They all mean 'stupid.' Look, I'll show you."

Beegee unwrapped the newspaper covering the thesaurus. He had marked the place with his bus pass. The others craned over his shoulders and jostled each other for a better look, except for Fuzzle and Henry. Fuzzle stood in the sinks. Henry stayed by the door, away from the buckets.

"See." Beegee pointed as he read. "'*Brainless, feeble-minded, weak in the upper story.*'"

"'*Nutty, sappy, spoony, doltish, asinine,*'" continued Thelma.

"'*Men of Gotham.*' Gotham? That's Batman!" said Willie.

"Gosh, Beegee. You have to be pretty smart to remember all those words," said Jonathan.

"Maybe you'll get promoted to E Group," said Grace.

"Or expelled," muttered Amanda.

"Hey, super book!" exclaimed Thelma. "I call it for tonight."

"Why you?" asked Grace. "We all want a turn." She looked at Willie.

"Thelma gets it," Willie decided.

"That's not fair," said Grace. "Why Thelma?"

Because, thought Willie, I like her.

"Because," said Willie, "she stole it."

4

THE MOMENT THELMA got home, even before she had a chance to take off her parka, she knew there was trouble.

Her mother was in the kitchen talking to someone. Her sharp voice could be heard clearly in the hall.

"All right. The joke's over. It's not funny anymore. Where is that baby? I want to know this instant!"

Thatcher, thought Thelma. He's at it again. A five-year-old brother was bad enough without having one who hid his wet bed sheets in the toy box and buried his vitamin pills in the sugar bowl.

Her mother's voice began again, pleasant and coaxing this time. "Now, sweetie, you're such a good looker and maybe it's Mommy's fault the baby is lost. But you'll help me find her, won't you, like my big boy?"

There was no answer. Thelma heard a chair scrape and her mother's prowling footsteps. Cupboard doors opened and shut and then her mother hurried into view, stooped over and searching. She peered up and down the hall.

"Thelma, thank heavens you're home. You will not believe what your brother's done."

"Yes I will," said Thelma.

"He's hidden the baby, again, because I wouldn't play firemen with him after lunch. And I still haven't finished repotting the plants."

"But I'm supposed to take her out in the carriage for you," said Thelma.

"And, of course, he won't tell me where," her mother babbled on. "She isn't in any of his usual hiding places and I can't think of where else to look. My head is splitting. Try the laundry hamper. No, wait—where was it he hid his pork chop that time? No, it couldn't be there. Maybe he put her in the hall closet." She opened the closet door and scrabbled through the winter coats.

"Don't be dense, Ma. He never puts anything in the closet."

"You're absolutely right. Why do I always get hysterical? Why can't I stay calm?" She turned toward the kitchen. The back of her skirt was wrinkled. Poor Ma, thought Thelma. Being a mother was hard enough without Thatcher. He made it impossible.

"Now, dearie," Thelma heard her mother say briskly, "baby is probably wet and hungry and we don't want that, do we?"

"Why not?" said Thatcher loudly.

Why not? thought Thelma. Because I like her. She's a girl and that makes two against one. Besides, there goes my baby-sitting money—that's why not.

"Now, now, Mommy knows you don't mean that, Thatcher. You may think you don't like the baby, but in your heart of hearts Mommy knows you love the baby."

"The baby stinks," said Thatcher. He marched into the hall wearing his Batman cape and a yellow helmet with a red plastic dome on the top that lit up. When he pressed the button by his right ear, the light inside the dome rotated and a siren wailed. His mother trailed after him.

"You feel that way now," she was saying, "but as soon as she can walk and talk you can play with her and show her how to run your racing cars." There was a pause. "Look what you're doing to me!" she yelled, her voice spiraling higher and higher. "You're making me shriek like a shrew. I'm dialing your father this very minute. He'll deal with you in two seconds flat!"

Thelma's brother pressed the button on his hat and disappeared into his room, light flashing and siren screaming. Her mother cast a despairing glance in Thelma's direction, flung her arms up helplessly, and followed him. Thelma hefted her pile of books, the thesaurus on top, and went after them. I'm never going to have any children, she thought. Her mother was trying to make herself heard over the *whaa whaa* of thc siren.

"I have an idea: I'll close my eyes and count to ten," said Thelma's mother, "and when I open them again I'll find you holding the baby. Okay? Here I go. One, two, three. . . ," she counted, ". . . eight, nine, ten. Ready or not—" and she opened her eyes.

Thatcher had put on his glasses with the windshield wipers attached to the frames and was rummaging through his desk.

"What in heaven's name are you doing now?"

"I'm looking for my bubble gum."

"Turn off that hideous noise!" his mother screamed. "You're a horrid, mean, wicked little boy!" She sank down on the bed. When she spoke again her voice was completely different—wheedling and sugary. "I'll buy you a whole new pack of bubble gum, darling, if you'll just tell me where you put the baby," she pleaded.

"I only like chewed gum," said Thatcher, his hat flashing like a lighthouse.

"What about a nice peanut-butter-and-marshmallow sandwich with no crusts—just the way you like them. I'll make you a whole plateful, if you'll find baby and bring her to mommy. But if you don't—" her voice rose to a screech— "you can forget about supper and breakfast tomorrow and lunch—" She stopped to catch her breath.

"I'm not hungry."

I'm going to be a forest ranger, thought Thelma, and live alone on top of a mountain with my radio and a television set and a dog. A dog would be nice.

Her mother rolled her eyes toward the ceiling. "I could kill him. I could absolutely kill him," she whispered to Thelma.

"Good idea," said Thelma encouragingly. She felt sorry for her mother. Her mother looked the way the fourth-grade teacher had looked when she discovered she was minus one kid after their class trip to the planetarium.

"Want me to try?" Thelma offered.

"Go ahead, though I don't know what good it will do. I'm going to take a couple of aspirin and call your father." Her mother stomped out of the room.

Thelma sat down on the bed and rested her chin on the top of her armful of books. What she really wanted was to bash her brother in the stomach until he doubled over, and then smash in his hat when he came up for air, and then bash him and smash him some more, and then have a cold Coke. No, it wouldn't work. He'd just scream at the top of his lungs and her mother would yell and the siren would whoop.

There would be too much noise to think. Then they'd never find the baby.

Thelma sighed. Thatcher had found his chewed wad of gum stuck to the side of one of the cubbyholes in his desk and was now softening it up. He chomped up and down while the windshield wipers swung back and forth and his hat flashed and wailed.

"Turn that thing off," said Thelma to see what he would do. Her brother smiled without opening his mouth and shook his head.

Okay, thought Thelma, I'll have to threaten him with something—something really terrible. Killing was good. But he'd heard it before. Her mother said it all the time. Something like killing, but better. Something new. But what? Then she remembered Beegee and the sixth-graders. She lifted her head from the stack of books. The thesaurus was right under her chin.

In a moment she was bent over the open book, reading. Every now and then she glanced at her brother and then went back to the page. She began to hum to herself and then to smile. When she looked up again she was laughing.

"What are you doing?" asked Thatcher.

"Reading," said Thelma loudly, so he'd be sure to hear her.

"Reading what?"

"This book." Her shoulders shook and she slapped her thigh. "This funny book."

"What's so funny?" His eyes, behind the windshield wipers, grew round.

"Ho, ho, ho, ha, ha, ha!" Thelma clutched her stomach and rocked back and forth. She glanced at her brother secretly to see if he was buying her act. "Haw, haw, haw." He edged closer. "Hee, hee, hee." Thelma lay on her back and kicked her legs in the air.

"What, Thelma? Tell me." The siren in his hat wailed.

"Here. Ho, ho, ho, hoo, hoo, hoo. Look right here."

Thelma tapped the page with one finger. Thatcher looked.

"I can't read," he said.

"Aaaah, ha ha, ha, too bad," shrieked Thelma, rolling onto the floor.

"Please, Thelma, read it."

Thelma pounded the floor with the open book. "Okay, hay, hay, hay. Give me your ha, ha, ha, hat first."

"Why?"

"Because," laughed Thelma, "I want to wear it while I read to you." He handed it to her. She put it on her head and turned the switch to OFF.

The silence was total. Thelma had stopped laughing. She got up off the floor, the book open in her hand.

"Why are you looking like that, Thelma?" asked Thatcher. "Read the funny part—you said."

"Okay," said Thelma. "I'll read you the good part, the part about what I'm going to do to you."

"Is that funny?"

"I think it's a riot," said Thelma. "Here, under *killing*. Did you know," she went on, "that your life hangs by a thread, your days are numbered, your hour has come, your doom is sealed? Did you know that you are about to have a fatal accident?"

"I don't care," said Thatcher. "Give me back my hat."

"Okay then," said Thelma smiling, "but maybe you'd care if you knew that I was going to murder you, bump you off, rub you out, launch you into eternity, and send you to join the heavenly chorus. Hmm. Let me see. I could strangle you, or throttle you. That's what they do to people who hide babies. It says it right here." Her brother frowned and put the tip of his thumb in his mouth. Thelma checked the book again. "Or I could do this, too: I could smother, drown, or behead you. Oooh—" she grinned at him nastily— "slitting your throat or burning you at the stake sounds fun. I like that." Thatcher took a step backward. His whole thumb had disappeared into his mouth. "Garrote might be too quick." Thelma closed the book with a snap. "I like this one best: If you don't tell me where the baby is right *now*, I'm going to cut you to pieces with a rusty razor blade and wade knee-deep in your blood."

Thelma took a step forward. Her brother stared up at her. "Okay, okay," he murmured.

Thelma followed him across the hall and through the kitchen. He opened the back door.

"Da, da, da," chortled the baby from under the fuzzy, pink blanket in the baby carriage.

"I was just getting her ready for you," said Thatcher meekly.

"And that's all there was to it," said Thelma in conclusion. She was standing between the clothesline and the sinks in the cleaning closet.

"Oh no, not quite. I forgot: besides the baby-sitting money, I also got a reward. Cash—five dollars on the spot. Well, actually, three dollars and twenty-five cents. That's all Mom had in her wallet. She's going to give me the rest today."

Wow, Thelma was tough and smart, Willie thought. "A book that makes money," he said aloud. "I'm glad I thought of stealing it."

"Glad I stole it, ya mean," said Thelma.

"Maybe Mrs. Dillworth won't notice it's missing after all," mumbled Amanda.

"Quit worrying, will ya, please," Willie told her.

"I gotta hand it to you, Thelma," exclaimed Grace. "I would have beaten him to a pulp, no matter what."

A bell clanged in the hallway.

"So who wants it next?" asked Willie.

"I do," said Jonathan quickly. He reached for the book.

"Now wait a minute," Grace began.

"I *need* it," Jonathan explained, "for my father."

"Okay. Jonathan's turn." Willie handed him the thesaurus and thought to himself: if Grace says one more word . . . but Grace didn't. Nobody did.

5

JONATHAN SLIPPED OUT of the cleaning closet ahead of the others, the book hidden under his jacket. He wanted to get away quickly before Grace could start whining about her turn again.

When he got downstairs, he put the book in his briefcase, snapped the catch shut, and locked it. He decided to keep his briefcase with him for the rest of the day. Now that he had the book, he didn't want to take a chance on losing it or having it disappear. There was something about this book—he didn't know what, exactly. It had helped Beegee and Thelma and it might, it just might, help his father. I bet it could work, he thought, but he knew if it were going to, it would have to work fast.

He was on his way to Current Events when he saw Mrs. Dillworth. She spotted him at the same moment and made straight for him. His first and only thought was to get by her as quickly as possible, but she blocked his way.

"Oh, Jonathan," she said, "I've been looking for someone, anyone, in O Group. My but you're hard to find!"

"Hard to find?" said Jonathan. He looked down without moving his head. The briefcase was still locked.

"A certain valuable reference book has disappeared from the library. The librarian discovered it was missing this morning and I couldn't find it on our special-reading table," Mrs. Dillworth continued.

"Our special-reading table?" said Jonathan. Very, very slowly he switched his briefcase to the hand farther away from Mrs. Dillworth.

"Yes. And I remember as if it were yesterday giving Willie permission to use it. It may be a shot in the dark, but I was wondering if, by mistake, one of you might have carried it off," said Mrs. Dillworth. Her eyes were fixed on his face.

"Carried it off?" said Jonathan, avoiding her stare. He concentrated on maneuvering the briefcase around behind him little by little. He hoped he was wider than it was.

"Yes. Carried it off," said Mrs. Dillworth. A teacher passed them, pushing a rolling cart. The jars on the cart clinked and rattled. Mrs. Dillworth's eyes never wavered. "The librarian refuses to blame me, but I feel totally responsible. I simply won't rest until I run it to ground."

"What does that mean?" asked Jonathan.

"Find it and return it to the library," said Mrs. Dillworth. "The sooner the better. This kind of loss will not be tolerated. Please speak to the others about it, dear. Immediately! Willie, in particular."

Mrs. Dillworth headed for the stairwell. Jonathan

watched her until her linty gray skirt and skinny legs had disappeared from sight. Then he ran.

He spoke to Willie before Current Events began. Willie was sitting on his desk with his feet in his chair zinging rubber bands across the room. Jonathan repeated what Mrs. Dillworth had said, word for word. "The thesaurus was in my briefcase, right under her nose, the whole time," he added. "And I have the feeling she's looking for you, too."

"I can handle her," said Willie. "You just hang on to the book. But play down Dillworth when you tell the others, especially Amanda."

Willie sounded very confident, but Jonathan's palms were still sweaty. He went to his seat and put his briefcase down. How was he going to tell Amanda without letting his worry show? He was trying to work out a way when Thelma was called on to read her current event. Then he was reminded of his other big problem.

Thelma stood up, a clipping from the *Daily Sun* in her hands. " *'The federal government today extended the time limit on emission controls for new cars . . .'* " was as far as she got.

"Cars shouldn't be allowed in cities anyway," interrupted Beegee. "Only bicycles."

"And skateboards," said Fuzzle.

"And horses," added Amanda.

Jonathan touched the briefcase with his foot. He forgot about Mrs. Dillworth completely. Instead he remembered the time he saw the mayor's car. It was long and black—very long, with an antenna and a flag and a siren. His father told him it had a telephone and an icebox, too. Once his father had run in a primary election for mayor. That car would have been fun. . .

Jonathan's thoughts were so far away from Current

Events that everybody was gathering up books before he realized the class was over. And in study hall, he stared at his open book without reading a word. He thought about the meeting set for that night. It wouldn't start until after supper. That would give the thesarus a little more time. Jonathan crossed two fingers on his left hand. Behind him, Amanda was whispering to Grace—something about angora sweaters.

"And diamond barrettes," whispered Amanda.

"I've seen those in the five-and-ten," Grace whispered back. "My mother promised to get me some for Christmas."

"I mean real ones," said Amanda. "The kind that come in black-velvet boxes. Mine cost hundreds."

Everything Amanda owned cost hundreds or thousands or millions, thought Jonathan. She was always letting you know how rich she was. It wasn't fair. He remembered suggesting to his father once that all the rich people should give half their money to the poor people so that everyone would be even. That was the year his father ran for state senator and talked more than usual about poverty. Willie and Beegee and some other kids had come to the campaign office to help pass out buttons and balloons. Jonathan's father had invited them to the victory party—only there hadn't been one. Jonathan remembered how gray the campaign office had looked late in the night and how few people had stayed after the returns came in. He remembered wandering across the littered floor, kicking at the balloons that had floated down from the ceiling. Balloons didn't look right on the floor. He tightened his stomach and bent over his book.

Jonathan didn't stay to play roof ball after school. He was cutting across the playground when he passed Henry, who was down on all fours just inside the gate.

"Bottom busted." Henry pointed to his torn shopping bag. His books, sneakers, and snacks were all over the ground. Henry was the only kid Jonathan knew who carried his things in a shopping bag.

"Doesn't matter," Henry said to himself, "I've got tons more of these bags at home. Oh—a Reese's Peanut Butter Cup! I'd forgotten I had this!"

Henry sat back on his heels and began to pick the lint and fuzz off the candy.

Jonathan kept on going. He knew where that ton of shopping bags had come from. His father had passed out hundreds of them when he ran for councilman—they had his name printed on them. The day after Jonathan's father lost the election, Henry had asked for all the leftovers.

Jonathan looked back. Henry was struggling to build a pile of his stuff. I should help him, thought Jonathan—but Henry might remember where the shopping bags had come from too. Jonathan ducked his head and ran for the bus.

Jonathan jumped down the steps of the bus at his stop and hurried up the street, his head lowered. As he turned the corner of his block, he slowed and then stood still. Maybe they weren't as bad as Mrs. Givens said. He raised his head and looked at the two trees in the middle of the block, one on each side of the street. There they were, thin and sick, with blotchy trunks and shriveled leaves. Mrs. Givens was right. She'd said all along that the trees ought to be cut down and replaced. Then she'd written a campaign letter promising to buy new ones with her own money if she were elected president of the block association.

Jonathan had seen the letter. He had picked it up off the doormat that morning. And there were envelopes just like it on all the doormats on his floor in the apartment building. Every person on the block must have gotten one. She was right. It was a good issue; Mrs. Givens was probably going to get elected. His father kept talking about being "your brother's keeper." It meant being neighborly, but Jonathan wasn't sure how many people understood that. His father would lose again, and then what would be left for him to run for?

A squashed beer can lay near the empty trash basket. Jonathan started to kick it down the block, pretending it was Mrs. Givens. The can rolled to a stop against the crust of a piece of pizza. With his toe he flipped it up and over the crust. It rolled through a yellow puddle at the base of a lamppost and made parallel tracks beyond. He watched it pass half an orange rind and topple off the curb into the gutter.

This street is a mess, thought Jonathan in disgust. He eyed a whole hot-dog roll with the mustard still on it and a piece of cellophane. After that came a squashed egg carton and one, no two, no three empty cigarette packs. There was an envelope and a candy-bar wrapper and a cigar stub—or worse: dog poop, he thought. Pages of newspaper were caught against the fencing around Mrs. Givens's sick trees.

"The whole block is a mess," he said out loud. "It's gross—really gross!"

He examined the sidewalk in front of him. Leaves from the tree lay scattered all around, mixed with bits of glass. A shattered bottle lay near the wall of one of the buildings. Light glinted off the blue-green slivers. Little kids could hurt themselves on that, he told himself.

Jonathan carefully inspected the last half of his block, between the tree and his awning. Besides paper everywhere he found one glove, a blue rag that looked a lot like a T-shirt, and, in front of his door, a tattered umbrella—inside out, with no handle. The handle was in the gutter, next to a bitten bagel, some eggshells, and a squashed sardine can.

"Yuck! Somebody's garbage . . . sick."

He suddenly smiled going up in the elevator.

"Filthy dirty," he announced inside his front door. "Hey, Dad?"

No one answered.

Jonathan checked the low bowl on the table under the mirror in the front hall. It was a habit. His mother used to leave notes for him there when she was going to be late, to tell him where she was and when she'd be back. It was still the first place he looked when he came home, even though his mother had died over a year ago and the bowl was always empty now.

I'd better get busy, he thought. He went into his room and set the briefcase on the floor beside his desk. He opened his file drawer and took out a new yellow legal pad. All the pencils in the mug were needle sharp. He picked one and lined it up beside the pad. Then, bending over, he unlocked his briefcase.

Jonathan heard the front door open and close. He looked up and was surprised to see his reflection in the window. When had it gotten dark? When had he turned on the light? What time was it?

"Jonathan. I'm home."

"Hi, Dad. I'll be there in a minute." He wasn't quite ready.

His father was sitting with his feet up and a drink in his hand when Jonathan burst into the living room.

"Dad! I have a great idea! Much better than Mrs. Givens's trees!"

His father's glasses were on his forehead and he was massaging the bridge of his nose.

"It must be a winner then," he said. The glasses slid back into place.

"It's about our street," said Jonathan. "It's offensive, abominable. . ." he looked down at the yellow pad, "putrid, and fetid." He smiled at his father.

"What? It's what?"

"Our street—it's a dog's dunghill, covered with offal, garbage, dregs, swill, and smudge!"

"Swill and smudge?"

"Yes. It's awful. People smirch, slubber, pollute, and sully. You should say that tonight, before the voting. Make it your issue."

"You mean at the meeting?"

"Yes."

"Is it really that bad?" asked his father, sitting forward in his chair.

"It's worse," said Jonathan. "You don't notice it so much because it's dark when you come home. And besides, you're much taller than me. I'm closer to the ground, so I see it better."

His father looked up at him.

"Do you think that a cleanup campaign would appeal to people?" he asked after a moment.

"More than trees, Dad. What good are new trees on a scurfy block?"

"No good," said his father. "You're right! Now that I think of it, the block has been going downhill recently." He looked at his watch. "It's worth a try. What were those words again?"

Jonathan handed him the pad.

"Here, look. And I can get more if you want them. I have a book."

Jonathan's father pulled on the knot of his tie and unbuttoned the top button of his shirt. *"Scurfy. Slubber. Smirch.* We can start with these," he said. "And you know more?" Jonathan nodded. "Hungry?"

"Not very," said Jonathan.

"Have an olive," said his father. He held out his glass. Three olives lay at the bottom. Jonathan fished one out. It tasted sour and good.

"And he won, right?" said Willie.

"No," said Jonathan. "Actually he didn't. Mrs. Givens did."

"Darn it!" Thelma slammed her fist against the wall of the cleaning closet. The rags on the clothesline jiggled.

"Mrs. Givens can go you-know-where," said Grace fiercely.

Willie didn't know what to say. Jonathan had been smiling all morning. He was smiling now. It didn't figure.

"She won because my father let her," said Jonathan.

"Let her?" said Willie.

"It was a tie," Jonathan explained. "But Mrs. Givens went on and on about how she'd been treasurer for seven years and she kept blowing her nose and sniffling. So my father withdrew and let her have it."

"I think that was very nice of your father," said Amanda, winding her gold chain around her finger.

"Yeah," said Willie. Jonathan's father was a bigger nincompoop than he'd thought.

"Nice guys always finish last," said Thelma.

"Not this time," said Jonathan. "The sanitation commissioner was at the meeting and he thought my dad's speech about cleaning up the block was terrific. He wants Dad to be chairman of a citywide campaign to make people stop littering. And my father said he'd do it—on one condition. The condition is us.

"Us?" said Amanda. "I don't litter and my governess doesn't like me to get dirty."

"Would she like you to get famous?" asked Jonathan. "Because that's what might happen. My father's going to put posters up all over—in buses and subways and storefronts, everywhere. And he said he couldn't do it without me, because of all the words I could find. I told him I had a lot of friends who could help and he said, 'They're hired!'"

"What do we have to do?" asked Fuzzle.

"Think up slogans for the posters. If my father uses one, the person who thought it up gets his or her name printed on the poster too."

"Tell me the words again," said Fuzzle.

Jonathan unlocked his briefcase and took out the thesaurus.

"I thought up 'Don't Slubber, Sweep!'" he said.

"*Scurfy*," said Grace. "That would be a good name for a dog."

"Think later, you guys. The bell's rung," said Willie. "Henry, check the hall. See if anyone's coming."

"Especially Mrs. Dillworth," said Amanda. "Now she's put a note on the bulletin board under Lost and Found. Haven't you seen it? I could hardly bear to look at it. It makes me feel like a criminal."

"Don't look at it then," snapped Willie. Amanda was such a dizzard—no guts.

Grace was whispering to Jonathan.

"Sure," said Jonathan. "If it's okay with Willie."

Grace had the thesaurus in her hands. She stared at Willie with a strange expression on her face. She looks like she's going to cry, Willie thought. He didn't want to get into that.

"Fine by me," he said. He watched Grace stick the book under the front of her sweater and fold her arms tightly around it.

6

THE WIND WAS like a wall. Grace pushed against it, her chin buried in the collar of her jacket and her arms wrapped around her books. Her bangs were blown straight back, out of her eyes for once, but she didn't need to see where she was going. She knew the way by heart. One block down from the bus stop, right turn at the Federal Deposit and Loan Building, and two and a half blocks over. Grace hurried. She was late and the wind didn't help. It was like trying to run under water.

The sign with the bold, black letters spelling out THE NEST swung crazily. She opened the door, letting in a blast of cold, and then leaned her full weight against it to close it again. A bell jangled over her head. Grace wiped her runny nose on her sleeve and took a deep breath. A warm smell of fur and milk and cedar chips and ammonia enveloped her. Even if

I were blind, I'd know where I was, she thought. Even if I were blind and couldn't smell a thing, I'd still know. The ringing of the bell had set off a chorus of yelps and whines and scratches and chirps.

"Shut up, you guys," said a young man in blue-jean overalls as he came out of a back room.

"Hi, Tony."

"Oh, hiya, Grace." Tony greeted her without stopping. "Want to give me a hand with this tank?" He picked up one end of a hose and bent over the empty aquarium.

"Well, I don't have too much time." Grace gestured to the back of the shop with her head. "I just thought I'd say hi to the puppies."

"Sure, sure. See if they need fresh water." Tony turned the nozzle and began to spray the sides of the tank.

Grace put her books on the counter and started toward the back of the shop. She walked close to the left-hand wall, running her fingers across the wire-mesh doors on the top tier of cages. She stopped to let the Lhasa apso lick her fingers while she checked the cages underneath. Both poodles were there but the German shepherd was gone. Tony must have sold him that morning. For a moment she was sad but then she remembered how cramped he'd looked in the cage. His paws were as big as doughnuts. It was better.

She crouched to see the new cocker puppies. They were in the last cage on the bottom row, next to the Siamese kittens. Four of them huddled in a heap on the shredded paper. Their eyes were closed and their faces wrinkled—with worry, Grace thought. She pressed her hands against the mesh.

"Hi, pups," she said.

An eye opened. The stub of a tail twitched. One of

the puppies pushed away from the others and waddled through the paper. Grace felt a spot of cool, wet nose on her palm. It was the girl—the runtiest one and the bravest. Her coat was redder than the others and the fur on the end of her ears damp and curling. The puppy sat down in the paper and looked up at her, hopefully. There were two lighter patches, shaped like tears, over each eyebrow.

Grace noticed that the water bowl was almost empty and that the paper around it was damp and matted. She opened the door and transferred the puppies one by one to the playpen in the middle of the floor. Then she cleaned the cage and relined it with armfuls of paper shreds from a plastic bag in the storeroom. She let the water run in the sink until it was cold, filled the bowl, and put it back in the cage carefully so nothing spilled. When she was through she stood looking down at the three brothers tumbling and climbing over each other in the middle of the playpen. The girl snuffled around the edges, exploring. Grace reached in to pat her. The puppy wagged her whole behind, legs too, and made a little puddle in her excitement.

I don't want to leave, thought Grace. I want to stay here forever.

"What time is it?" she asked Tony.

"After four." The hose was looped around his shoulder. "Cage looks good, Grace. Thanks."

After four. Grace quickly put the puppies back. The boys trembled when she picked them up and flattened themselves against her chest, but the girl tried to climb onto her shoulder. She'd saved the girl for last. The puppy's bottom was damp but Grace didn't mind. She stroked the tiny dome of its head, smoothing back the extra folds of skin from the puppy's face.

"I have to go now," she whispered, "but I'll be back tomorrow."

The puppy watched her, very still, the whites of its eyes showing in half-moons above the dark brown pupils. Then the puppy stretched up and washed Grace's chin with its warm tongue.

Grace glanced up at the clock above the receptionist's desk at her mother's advertising agency. Forty-three minutes late. She nodded at the receptionist and walked as fast as possible, without actually running, down the long, carpeted hall and got a tremendous shock from the metal doorknob. She pushed open the office door and looked in.

Her mother stood at the corner of her desk, tilting slightly to the left to talk on the phone. She had buttoned her coat and her right arm curved around a stuffed briefcase and a stack of papers. She looked ready to leave for the day, but Grace knew she wasn't.

"Uh huh, uh huh, uh huh," her mother was saying into the phone. She mouthed a silent hello and her eyebrows went up and down in greeting. With a long nod of her head, she indicated that Grace was to sit down. Grace perched on the arm of a chair.

A few minutes later Grace took off her jacket and settled back into the cushions with her books in her lap. She had hidden the thesaurus in the middle of the pile in case she ran into Mrs. Dillworth on the stairs after dismissal. The word REWARD, in capital letters, had been added to the notice on the Lost and Found board and Mrs. Dillworth seemed to be lurking everywhere. She had caught and had questioned Willie twice. The first time she had repeated what they already knew, that she felt totally responsible for letting the thesaurus slip through her fingers, so to speak, and that even though the librarian was being very understanding, Mrs. Dillworth felt so guilty she could hardly bear to look her in the eye. The second time she'd put a hand on Willie's arm and said she was quite sure she remembered that he was the last one to have hold of the missing book. Willie pretended he was Fuzzle and innocently asked her if it was a book about dinosaurs. Thelma wasn't sure Dillworth had been fooled. She thought frisking might be next.

I'll look up *dog* now while I'm waiting, thought Grace. She was about to do it when her mother hung up.

"Oh! That man gives me a pain." She sank down into the desk chair and unclipped the earring on her left ear. "Gracie, love, I'm sorry. I really meant to be ready."

"Can we go now?" asked Grace.

"I've got a call coming. Just one more." Her mother checked the clock on her desk. "In about five minutes. A conference call. Shouldn't take too long. How was your day?"

"I stopped at the pet store. You know the one?"

"Your friend Tony's place? How could I forget?"

"They have a new litter of puppies."

"Another one?" Her mother picked up the earring on her desk and began to snap the clasp open and shut.

"Mom, the littlest one looked so sad when I left. I'm afraid if she stays there too long she's going to get kennel cough."

"Kennel what?"

"Even Tony's worried about her, Mom. She needs a mother."

"Oh, sweetie. We've been over that so many times."

"I know, but. . ."

"But nothing has changed. Daddy travels a lot. I'm gone all day. Mrs. Grimes doesn't come in until one o'clock in the afternoon. And she has enough to do without cleaning up after a dog."

"But I've thought it all out. I've figured out how it could work." Grace stood up and moved closer to her mother. A light flashed on the phone. They both saw it. Grace began to talk very fast.

"It'll work. I can do it. I can. No extra. . ." but her mother was listening to the receptionist's voice coming over the intercom:

"It's Mr. Cohen in Atlanta and Ms. Renshaw in Birmingham on extension eight."

"Oh, Mom. I haven't gotten to my good ideas," said Grace.

"Write me a memo." Her mother put one hand on the receiver and began to unbutton her coat with the other. "Give me your arguments in writing. I think better when I see things in black and white. You got some new ideas? Put 'em down." She shrugged her shoulders instead of saying any more and picked up the phone.

"Hello. Yes. Right."

Grace scooped up her books and jacket. Her mother was saying "uh huh, uh huh, uh huh" when Grace quietly closed the door. She carried her stuff down the hall.

The receptionist's chair was empty. Her desk was bare except for the telephone, with its rows of buttons, an electric pencil sharpener, and the IN and OUT boxes. Why not? thought Grace. She didn't know much about memos, but it was worth a try. She slid onto the chair. The best place to write one was at the kind of desk where memos got written. She twirled around in the chair twice to get ready. Then she opened her binder and stuck a pencil in the sharpener, feeling businesslike and confident.

MEMO she printed at the top of a clean page, and

under that, FROM GRACE. Better get right to the important part, she thought. Her mother didn't like people who wobbled and wavered.

"A puppy will not be a bother to anyone," she wrote, *"because:"* She numbered each point as she went along—it looked more serious.

1. I will get up at 6:45 A.M. and walk it.

2. I will walk it again after breakfast, just in case. I will do all the walking.

3. I will give it its breakfast.

4. I will buy, with my own money, squeaky toys and a clock with a loud tick that I will wrap in an old towel so that it will think its mother is near. Tony says the ticking sounds like a heartbeat.

5. It will be a small dog, not a Great Dane or Newfoundland like I asked for before. A cocker, maybe.

6. I will clean up after it. Everything.

7. I will buy soda water with my own money for the stains, just in case—even though there won't be any.

8. I will lay down newspaper everywhere.

9. I will pay Mrs. Grimes with my own money to give it a little pat and its lunch, which I will fix and put on the counter before I leave for school.

10. I will train the dog to sit, lie down, roll over, beg, fetch, play dead, jump through hoops (which I will buy with my own money), guard the house, and count like I've seen them do on TV by barking.

11. I will also train it not to whine cry, scratch at doors, snuffle up people's skirts, jump up on people (except burglars), chew things, and make mistakes.

12. I will buy with my own money a flea collar when it needs one.

Grace stretched the fingers on her writing hand and stuck the pencil into the sharpener again. She tossed her bangs back and began a new section.

A puppy will be fun for everyone because:

1. When Dad comes home from a trip it will lick his hands and face and bring his newspaper. Remember, I said I'd teach it to fetch.

2. It will be company for Mrs. Grimes.

3. When I come home, I can talk to it instead of Mrs. Grimes. I can also cuddle it and love it and kiss it.

The memo reached the bottom of the second page. Grace leaned on her elbows and, holding her bangs back with both hands, reread what she had written. Pretty good, she thought. If she were her mother that puppy would be out of The Nest by suppertime. But the trouble was, she wasn't her mother.

Grace pushed back the chair, got up, and walked away from the desk. She needed an ending. With her foot she traced the geometric pattern of the rug. Her mother would say it's gotta have "pow—" it's got to sweep them off their feet. Grace's foot stopped moving. The thesaurus! Of course—the thesaurus. She was back at the desk, sitting down, with the thesaurus open in front of her—all in one breath.

It took her ten minutes to find the words she wanted, and when she was through, all of the fingers on her left hand except her thumb marked places in the book that she needed.

"You see," she wrote, *"I want a dog. I am eager, avid, and keen to have a dog. I am hankering, yearning, and longing for one. My mouth is watering. I have set my heart upon it; I am dying for one."*

Grace smiled and flipped the pages to her middle finger. *"If we don't get a dog I will be more than sad: I will be crushed, dashed, defeated. My bubble will burst; my hopes will be blighted and slip between cup and lip."*

I think this will really, really do it, Grace thought as she opened to her fourth finger. *"My spirits will droop, my heart will sink, and my head will hang down. I will probably have the blues, dismals, dumps, and doldrums. Mopes and vapors, too."*

There was more. Grace turned the page with her little finger. She'd never written so much or so fast before. *"I might cry myself blind, grimace, gnash my teeth, tear my hair, roll on the ground, and burst with grief. But mostly I will be brokenhearted and forlorn."*

Grace read the whole memo over to herself. She checked the spelling, made some corrections—*breakfast* and *burglars*—and read it again. It got better and better. Why didn't I think of writing a memo before? she thought. Her mother couldn't say no now. No way. She gave the thesaurus a little pat. Willie was smart to think of stealing it. She could hardly wait to tell him in the morning.

The finished memo was three pages long. She gathered the sheets together and clicked them on the desk top to line them up. In the middle drawer she found a paper clip and slid it on.

This time she walked with determined steps back to her mother's office. At the opening of the door her mother swung around in the desk chair, the phone cradled between her cheek and shoulder. When she saw Grace she put both hands out, palms up. Grace crossed the carpet to the desk, laid the memo down, and tiptoed out of the room. She closed the door behind her, but not quite all the way. Through the narrow crack she watched her mother lean forward to look at the memo. Good. She was reading it. The sooner the better, thought Grace. The shop might still be open. Halfway down the first page her mother smiled. The smile grew wider. As she got to the top of the last page, she began to shake her head. She let out a noise like a snort and quickly covered the mouthpiece of the phone with her right hand. Then she leaned back in her chair and laughed and laughed.

Grace backed away from the door, her eyes stinging. Then she turned and ran, but the laughter followed her all the way down the hall.

"Why are we having the meeting anyway?" asked Fuzzle, catching up to Willie on the stairs. "Grace is absent and she's got the thesaurus."

Willie kept climbing. "I don't think she's absent," he said.

"Whataya mean, not absent? She sits right next to me and she wasn't there. Her chair was empty."

"She's gone—split!" said Thelma, joining them on the landing. "Remember English? They asked if we knew where she was. The whole school's looking for her. I bet they've got the cops in on it too."

A bunch of kids plodded up the stairs toward them. Willie edged closer to the railing to let them pass. He remembered times when he wished that Grace would bug off or break a leg or drop dead or something. He didn't wish it now.

Fuzzle peered down the stairwell. "Wait," he said, "here come the others."

Willie leaned next to him. A flight below they could see Henry's pudgy hand as he hauled himself up by the railing. He was the last one to reach the landing. Figures, thought Willie, but he didn't give Henry a chance to rest.

"Come on," he said. "I haven't got all day."

They slipped into the cleaning closet and closed the door. Willie heard Henry panting in the dark. He turned on the light.

Someone was sitting on a bucket next to the sink. It looks just like Grace, thought Willie in a flash—but it couldn't be. His hand seemed stuck to the light switch. He glanced at the door and then back again. It was Grace all right, with her shirt hanging out and

her knee socks rolled down on top of her sneakers. She was blinking at him, one hand raised to shield her eyes. Willie switched off the light. He couldn't think of anything else to do.

"It's Grace!" said Beegee in the dark.

"Where?" asked Fuzzle.

"Right in front of you," said Jonathan.

Someone brushed against Willie's shoulder. The light went on again. Grace hadn't moved. Her face was all screwed up and creased below her bangs, and one of her ponytails had come undone.

"You okay, Grace?" asked Thelma.

Grace rubbed her nose and glared at Willie with red-rimmed eyes.

"What happened to you?" said Amanda. "You look absolutely awful."

"Shut up, Amanda," said Thelma.

"What are you doing here?" asked Fuzzle. "You're supposed to be missing."

"Are you sick?" asked Beegee.

Grace bent over without answering. Her jacket and sweater and books were piled on the floor at her feet. She picked up one of the books and held it out. It was the thesaurus.

"You see this?" Her voice sounded rusty. "Well, it can go you-know-where. It pukes!" The thesaurus slammed to the floor. "And besides, I hate it!"

"Keep your voice down," said Amanda.

"I did everything the other guys did." Grace was almost shouting now and was pointing at Willie at the same time. "I even wrote all the words down—and you know what happened? My mother laughed! Just laughed. She thought it was funny." Grace's finger stopped poking the air and her lips shut tight.

I didn't make her take it, thought Willie. She wanted it from the first. He was about to remind her, but now Grace was doing something else. Something worse. She was crying.

"It's all right, Grace," said Fuzzle. "Don't cry. You're not absent. The cops can stop looking for you."

"Don't be so idiotic all the time, Fuzzle. Of course she's not absent," said Amanda. "You're getting your skirt all wet, Grace."

"I don't care," sobbed Grace.

"Where have you been?" asked Thelma

"Here," said Grace. She wiped her face with her fists.

"In the cleaning closet?" asked Amanda.

"No." Grace snuffed twice and swallowed. "They use the mops and waxers after school. So I hid in the bathroom until they'd gone. I stood on the toilet so they couldn't see my feet under the door."

"You spent all night on the toilet?" said Jonathan.

"No. I lay on a mat in the gym."

They stared at her in silence. Willie tried to picture the gym at night, empty and black, with just the moonlight coming in through the high windows and spooky shadows everywhere. In the dark the hanging rings and ropes must have looked like nooses. I would have been scared to death, he thought.

"It was so cold," Grace added, "I kept my jacket on."

"Staying out all night was a mean thing to do!" said Amanda. "Your mother is absolutely frantic. I know. She called my governess."

"Amanda," said Thelma slowly, "stuff it."

"I don't even care if she's dead," said Grace. "She laughed. That's what she did—*laughed.*"

"What did you mother think was so funny?" asked Beegee.

"My memo," said Grace. She began to cry again, but not as hard as before. Between pauses to wipe her nose and catch her breath, she told them about the new litter of cocker puppies and then what happened in her mother's office. "It isn't fair. It wasn't funny—it was serious."

"Maybe she wasn't laughing at you," said Fuzzle.

"Yes, she was. It was *my* memo."

"Dogs are nicer than people, sometimes," said Thelma.

"I wish we could have a dog," said Fuzzle, "but my father's allergic and so am I."

Amanda adjusted her barrettes and cleared her throat.

"I'm sorry to disagree, Grace," she said, "but your mother is absolutely right. I know. I have dozens of dogs. Purebreds—Bedlington terriers and some cockers, too, I think—but we keep them in our kennel in the country. My mother says they're much happier there. She says an apartment is no place for a dog, even if it's toilet-trained."

"Cut it out, Amanda," said Willie. He wanted to gag her with a mop. Or strangle her with a dirty rag. He glanced at Thelma.

"I'm just trying to help," said Amanda. "Maybe Grace can come to my country house for the weekend and see all my puppies." She bent toward Grace. "You can pat them as much as you like."

Grace began to cry again.

"Gee, Amanda, that's nice. Really terrific." Willie had never heard Jonathan speak so sarcastically before. "What a super friend you are.

"And what does that mean, may I ask?" said Amanda.

"Figure it out," said Willie.

Thelma turned her back on Amanda. "Hey, Grace, you must be starving."

Grace sat slumped on her bucket. "I stole some saltines from the lunchroom this morning, very early," she said in a low voice.

"I've got a few snacks in my locker," said Henry.

"Lots of chocolate bars and a whole bag of barbecue potato chips. You can have everything."

"I'll take your books," offered Willie. "Check the hall, Fuzzle."

"I can't go," said Grace.

"Don't worry," said Thelma, "we'll go with you."

Beegee picked up Grace's jacket and sweater and handed them to her. No one looked at Amanda.

"Okay," said Fuzzle, "I think there's nobody there."

"I may have some chocolate-chip cookie pieces, too," said Henry, smiling at Grace. "Homemade." He held the door open.

"What about Mrs. Dillworth's thesaurus?" said Amanda. "You can't just leave it here on this filthy floor."

"You take it," said Willie, over his shoulder. "I guess it's your turn."

7

MY TURN. AMANDA looked at the book on the floor. Who did Willie think he was, taking off and leaving her with stolen property, after she'd told him a dozen times how bad Mrs. Dillworth's notices made her feel? It was so unfair. Besides, I should be with Grace, she thought. I've told her we're best friends, and she really needs me at a time like this. I'll bet she doesn't even have a dime for the phone.

The others had left the door wide open. Any moment someone might come along and see her standing all alone with the mops and pails as if she were weird or something.

Amanda bent down hurriedly and picked up the thesaurus. No matter what, books should not be left on the floor. She gave the front and back covers a quick brush and stepped out of the closet, closing the door firmly behind her.

Now, how do I hide this thing? she thought, halfway down the first flight of stairs. If I put it under my sweater it will stretch it out of shape, and baggy angora makes me look fat. And I'm certainly not going to squeeze it between my legs like Thelma did.

She tucked it under her arm instead, the front cover against her side. Most of the book still showed.

"I'll be so mad if I get caught," Amanda grumbled to herself. "I absolutely refuse to take the blame. I was the one who *told* them it was wrong." She paused, thinking. I'll return it—that's what I'll do. Without telling them. That will serve them right and Mrs. Dillworth will be so pleased and grateful. I'll put it back on the table in the library. She turned to retrace her steps and then stopped again. No. Not now. After I've seen about Grace. After school.

She continued down the stairs, wondering what sort of reward Mrs. Dillworth had in mind. Whatever it is, I deserve it, thought Amanda.

But how will she know it was me? Oh, blither! She won't. Amanda stopped on the landing between the fifth floor and the fourth. Just putting the book back would be sneaky. Much better to walk right up to Mrs. Dillworth, look her straight in the eye, and say that I found it on the floor. Amanda smiled. "On the floor," she said to herself out loud.

Quick footsteps clicked on the flight of steps above her head. Someone was coming down the stairs at top speed. Amanda looked over her shoulder. Yorks! It was Mrs. Dillworth, of all people. She heard me, thought Amanda. She's after me! Amanda jumped the next steps two at a time, reached the next landing, and rounded the corner. Not now, she thought—I'm not ready. She glanced back. Mrs. Dillworth was gaining on her. It didn't seem possible that a teacher could move that fast, especially in high heels. The thesaurus slipped against Amanda's sweater and she had to hike it up as she ran. From the sounds following her, Mrs. Dillworth's shoes seemed to be growing larger and larger.

"I'm done for!" gasped Amanda to herself, scuttling down the next flight. It's all their fault. I can't go any faster. I'll fall and break my nose.

"Yoo-hoo, yoo-hoo," Mrs. Dillworth was calling. She was right behind her now. There was no point in running anymore. It was hopeless. She was trapped. The windows had wire mesh over them even. Amanda stopped suddenly and turned to face her. "Hi, Mrs. Dillworth," she blurted. "I was looking all over for you." She held out the book.

Mrs. Dillworth hardly paused. "Oh, Amanda dear—have you heard the good news about Grace? I'm on my way to the lobby."

"I found this," said Amanda, "a few floors back." She swung the book in a curve as Mrs. Dillworth brushed past her and clattered on ahead. "Later, dear, later." Amanda let her hands drop. Her knees felt weak, as if they might give way at any moment. She waited for a few minutes and then she continued down, carrying the thesaurus.

The main floor looked like it did during the early morning rush. A crowd of people, including the principal and both fifth-grade teachers, was milling about in front of the nurse's office. Mrs. Cleft had even come up from the kitchen carrying a can the size of a wastebasket in her arms—something red. Stewed tomatoes or beets, thought Amanda.

In the center of all the commotion stood Grace. Someone had combed her hair and redone the elastics on her ponytails. Grace didn't look as sick as before and there was a bulge in one of her cheeks. Amanda knew it was a sour ball. The nurse gave out more sour balls than aspirins. Probably cherry, thought Amanda. Grace tilted her head back to let the nurse put another bobby pin in her bangs, then licked her lips with a green tongue.

Thelma and the others were gathered around her in a half-circle. Henry had bulges in both cheeks and his mouth was working. The principal was listening to Willie. Amanda figured from the gestures he was making that he must be describing Grace's night alone in the school. Occasionally he glanced at Grace. Grace sucked on her sour ball. Once in a while she nodded.

Amanda stood on the fringes of the crowd, near the front door. She wished someone would notice she was there and say something to her, but no one did. I could fall down in a dead faint on this hard floor and have a concussion, she thought, and that nurse would go right on patting Grace's head.

Amanda wanted to go home. But just then Grace's mother pushed through the front door and stood looking around uncertainly.

"Hello," said Amanda. She tapped Grace's mother on the arm. "You must be here for Grace." Grace's mother didn't seem to recognize her. She must be too worried.

"I can explain everything," Amanda went on. "I told Grace you were frantic." There was so much noise, she had to repeat it. "I said, I told Grace you were frantic."

Grace's mother stared in confusion at the crowd around the nurse's office. She took a few steps forward. Amanda stuck close beside her.

"I said: 'Grace, that was a mean thing to do to your mother!'" Amanda glanced up to see if she had been heard this time. It was hard to tell.

Grace's mother moved forward quickly. She lifted one arm and waved. Her purse banged Amanda on the head.

"Then I said," Amanda continued, even louder, "Your mother is *absolutely* right."

Grace's mother pushed through the crowd. Amanda caught a glimpse of her kneeling with her arms around Grace before people got in the way.

"You said, you said! We all know what *you* said," Willie hissed.

Amanda started. He was so close he was almost touching her.

"Why don't you shut up and think about Grace for a change?" Willie went on.

"I think about her all the time," said Amanda. "She's my best friend."

"Boy, I'm glad I'm not," cracked Thelma, joining them.

"Hah! Enemy's more like it. You don't even know what friend means," said Willie. "And you're brainless, too. Gimme that."

Willie snatched the book out of her hand. Amanda had forgotten she had it and had been holding it out in the open where anyone could have seen it.

"You can't be trusted with anything, can you?" accused Willie. "What were you planning to do? Give it back?"

"It would be just like her," agreed Jonathan.

Willie concealed the book under his shirt and turned toward the stairs. Amanda looked around to see if anyone had heard them. Grace and her mother and the principal had disappeared. The teachers were herding the others back to their classrooms. Only Mrs. Dillworth and Mrs. Cleft were left. Mrs. Dillworth glanced at Amanda and smiled. Amanda looked down. She couldn't think of anything to say to Mrs. Dillworth right at the moment.

For the rest of the day Amanda hardly said a word, but she knew, she just *knew*, they were all talking about her. To everyone. Even in the bathroom. She heard

Thelma come into the cubicle next to hers with someone whose shoes she didn't recognize. First they whispered and then they laughed. Amanda felt like crying. She considered wriggling out under the side partitions at the end near the door—but you never knew what might be on the bathroom floor. So she waited—for ages—until they left.

All the rest of O Group were sitting together at lunch when she got there. They had piled their trays on the only chair left. Amanda had to carry her tuna goo and beet salad to a table full of disgusting fourth-graders, who spent the whole time mashing their food together and then drowning it in milk.

After lunch, O Group disappeared. All through Art Amanda dribbled water on her clay pot and wondered where they were. Maybe in the cleaning closet. Maybe voting her out. Then where could she go? Home, thought Amanda. I want to go home to Mamzelle.

Mamzelle, in her everyday red wool coat with the fur collar, was waiting by the gate when school let out. A flock of pigeons pecked and cooed on the pavement near her. When she saw Amanda she scattered the last of the bread crumbs and shooed the pigeons away from her feet.

"Oh, Zelly!" said Amanda, throwing her arms around her. "I'm so glad to see you.

Zelly tottered and then righted herself. Her button face beamed and she bustled and bobbed inside Amanda's hug.

"'Allo, 'allo, ma petite." She patted Amanda's scarf and felt her cheeks. Amanda could smell the lotion on her hands.

"You are flushed, my pigeon." Zelly touched the inside of her wrist to Amanda's forehead. "A fever? Non. Just too much fun. And now, the roulettes?"

Mamzelle held up a pair of roller skates. "Or the bicyclette?"

"Bicycle. It's faster. I want to get out of here." She handed Mamzelle her schoolbag. Her bike was leaning against the fence. Zelly had already undone the lock. As Amanda started off, Zelly called out her usual stream of cautions.

"Pas vite, ma chère, not too fast. Attention at the lights. Guard against the autos. There are very many fools driving around."

Usually Amanda rode slowly so Zelly could keep up, but today she pedaled faster and faster, leaving Zelly and her warnings far behind. She had already washed her hands and face and was curled up on her canopied bed clicking her TV's remote control from channel to channel when Mamzelle appeared, panting, in the doorway.

"Oh, my lamb!" She put a hand on her heart and her eyes rolled up. "My legs, they don't run like they used to." She took a deep breath. "Never mind. We have tea, yes?"

"No," said Amanda. "I don't want any."

"Tiny, tiny little tartelettes, with strawberry jam—some with custard and cinnamon on top. Hummm?" Zelly smacked her lips.

"Okay," said Amanda, pressing another button.

"Très bien. You rest, my pet. I'll bring it here."

Zelly disappeared. There was nothing good on TV. Amanda pressed all the buttons again just to make sure and then turned it off. She sat staring at the blank gray square of the screen, with the remote control still in her hand. TV was a bore. There was never anything good on. There was a stack of records next to the stereo, and her collection of perfume bottles and glass animals glittered on the dressing table. But she felt too tired to get up. She wished Zelly would come back. Maybe she was hungry after all. She wished Zelly would hurry.

From down the hall she heard the tinkle of the tea tray and the *pork-pork* sound of Zelly's heels on the tile floor.

"Voilà!" said Zelly, setting the tray down on the table in front of the window seat. "Come. Sit. We talk about your birthday. She is less than a month away." Zelly poured two cups of tea from the silver pot, added sugar and a sliver of lemon, and passed one to Amanda. "Shall we rent the ferryboat again or have the party here?"

"Here, I guess. I don't care. It doesn't matter—no one will come."

"But of course they will come, lovekin. They always come. We will have prizes, glorious prizes, and the favors—fantastique." Mamzelle bunched the fingers of one hand together. Her eyes crossed as she kissed the tips loudly and then flung her hand in the air, fingers outstretched. "Silver dollars in the cake, miniature soldiers in walnut shells, gold rings in marshmallows—"

"Zelly." Mamzelle was going off into one of her dramatic spells. "You don't understand. Nobody likes me."

"— baseball mittens and cameras instantmatique. . ."

"Stop, Zelly. It isn't the prizes. I don't have any friends."

"Friends. No friends?" Zelly's teacup rattled in her saucer.

"That's what I've been trying to tell you."

"Well—so, pouf, phooey, who needs friends?" Zelly set her cup on the tray so she could talk with both hands. "You have beauty and your talent. You have little feet and tiny ears and big money and all your clothes are imported from Paris, the city of lovers . . .

There, there, my sweet, my caramel, my bonbon, don't cry." But Amanda's tears kept spilling over and the last bite of strawberry tart stuck in her throat. She felt the teacup being taken out of her hands and Zelly's soft pats on her back.

"You have friends, chérie," said Zelly, wiping Amanda's cheeks with a tea napkin. "There is always me."

"I know that, but I don't mean someone old."

"And," Mamzelle went on, "there's Weelie and Zelma and that boy, Fuddle."

"That's not true. They won't even talk to me."

"Non, non. You are mistaken. They gave me a present for you, after you departed on the bicyclette. I almost forgot. Wait."

Zelly was back in a moment, carrying something wrapped in blue and white cloth. Amanda recognized it as the top of Fuzzle's sweat suit. "And they said they would give you something else," said Zelly encouragingly, "if you forget to bring it back tomorrow. So nice. So kind. . ." She put the bundle in Amanda's lap.

Amanda eyed the lumpy package doubtfully. She had heard about people sending garbage disguised as gifts. Zelly popped a tartelette into her mouth and picked up the tea tray.

"Why do you wait? Unwrap it, ma chére," she prompted. "Oh, I see. A sweaty suit. Icky poo-poo." She wrinkled her nose. "Never mind. I'll wash it later."

After Zelly had gone, Amanda sat without moving. At least it isn't ticking, she thought. She leaned over and sniffed. It didn't smell any worse than Fuzzle. Finally she untied the sleeves and unzipped the zipper.

It was only the thesaurus.

She picked it out of the folds of the sweat jacket and looked at it. A torn-off strip of lined paper stuck out from between the pages. Uh-oh, thought Amanda. An anonymous note. I won't read it.

She put the book on the window seat, but she couldn't take her eyes off the scrap of white paper. It tempted her, like a dare. Oh darn, I'll do it, Amanda thought, even if there's a mashed cockroach in there. She opened the book.

There was nothing written on the sliver of paper. It was merely there to mark the page—a page of *F* words. The word *friend* leaped up at her. It had been underlined in red pencil, and some of the words after it had a faint red line under them, too. Amanda read them all and then went back over them. Her eyes jumped from one underlined term to another as if the page were a checkerboard. *Buddy, messmate, pal, ally, amigo, sidekick, sympathizer,* and *friend in need.* She counted them. There were eight all—nine if she included *friend.* Her eyes stuck on *friend in need.* She remembered Grace in the cleaning closet, huddled and sad, with tears dripping from her cheeks and chin and spotting her skirt.

Zelly bustled in, humming to herself. She picked the sweat jacket off the window seat and held it out in front of her with two fingers.

"Now, you icky poo-poo thing," she said to the jacket, "I wash."

"Zelly, what is a friend in need?" Amanda looked up front the book.

"Trés simple," said Zelly. "If you know someone who has a need and you have the possibility to find out what it is and fix it, then you are the friend in need. You understand?"

Amanda sat very still, thinking. *Ally, sympathizer.* She read the words again. "Yes," she said suddenly. "Yes, I do." She jumped up and, grabbing Zelly's hands, danced her around in small circles; the sweat jacket flapped between them.

"Okay, Zelly, go tell the cook we'll need the picnic hamper. I'll order the car.

"Where are we going?" asked Zelly. "Shall I ask the cook to wrap the lamb chops in tinfoil?"

"Just the hamper. We don't need any food."

"A picnic. With no food?"

"We are not going on a picnic," said Amanda firmly.

"Where are they?" Willie drummed his fingers on the side of the bucket. "How long can one phone call take?"

"Quiet," warned Thelma. "I think I hear someone."

Willie flattened his hands on the bucket and cocked his head, listening. Outside in the hall he heard muffled shufflings and whispers and then the door opened part way and Amanda and Grace slipped into the cleaning closet.

" 'Bout time," said Willie under his breath. Amanda and Grace stood wedged together with their backs against the door. They'd been glued together all morning like Siamese twins, thought Willie. In one hand Amanda carried her schoolbag. At least she hadn't forgotten the thesaurus. Willie knew it was in there. He'd waited outside before school to ask her and she'd pointed to the bag and nodded.

"Sorry we're late," said Amanda. "We had to make a phone call."

"We know that." Willie hunched his shoulders and glared at her.

"Was your mother mad after she got you home, Grace?" asked Beegee.

Grace and Amanda looked at each other and giggled. One more giggle and it will be their last, thought Willie.

"Come on. Give," said Thelma. "I have to go to the bathroom."

"Shall we tell them, Amanda?" asked Grace.

"We'll give you a little hint," said Amanda. "Grace's apartment is absolutely covered with newspapers. Wall to wall."

"A puppy," gasped Henry. "That's got to mean a puppy!"

"Terrific, Grace!" said Thelma.

"A puppy," breathed Fuzzle. "Lucky you."

Grace was shaking her head and grinning.

"Wrong," said Amanda. A bell clanged in the hall. "Remember, I said *absolutely* covered!"

"You're painting the apartment?" guessed Fuzzle.

Grace leaned forward, her eyes gleaming. "Not *a* puppy, you boobies. *Puppies!* Two of them!"

"Two puppies?" said Henry.

"And one's from me," finished Amanda triumphantly.

"From you?" said Jonathan. He sounded as if he couldn't believe it.

"First came Scurfy," said Grace, "the cocker from the pet store. My mother and I went there straight from school. And then, late last night, the doorbell rang . . ."

"Let me tell," said Amanda. "And it was me and Zelly and Amigo. . ."

"In a picnic hamper," said Grace. "My mother didn't know whether to laugh or cry."

"What kind did Amanda bring you?" asked Jonathan. He sounded as if he still couldn't believe it.

"A purebred Bedlington terrier," Amanda told him.

"He feels like baby powder," said Grace, "and Amanda named him Amigo because he's going to be Scurfy's friend."

"Like me and Grace," said Amanda. She shot a quick glance at Willie. Don't look at *me*, thought Willie—it was Jonathan's red pencil.

"Zelly said they love each other already," Grace

continued. "We called her. She's at my apartment sitting with them until they get used to being alone."

The bell rang again.

"That's the second bell," said Jonathan.

"Everyone can come to my house after school," said Grace. "Okay, Amanda?" She started to open the door.

"Wait a minute. What about the thesaurus?" asked Willie.

"Oh, I almost forgot," said Amanda. "And this, too." She fished something else out of her schoolbag and handed it and the thesaurus to Fuzzle.

"What is it?" asked Fuzzle.

"Your sweat-suit top. I'm sorry about the starch. Zelly starches everything."

"It's stiff as a board," said Fuzzle in wonder.

"Stop complaining," said Willie, "and take the thesaurus, since you've already got it. Wrap it in the sweat suit."

"I can't. It won't bend," said Fuzzle.

"Figure out something," Willie told him. "But whatever you do, don't lose it."

8

ACROSS THE STREET the sun turned the sides of the buildings a warm gold, but it was cold in the shadow of the museum. Fuzzle was glad he'd decided to wear the top of his sweat suit; he didn't mind that sharp creases ran the length of the arms and the fold lines still showed like a tic-tac-toe across his chest.

He had left his books at school. Most of his homework was done anyway—if he didn't count the back assignments and the unfinished corrections piled at the bottom of his locker. But he was carrying the thesaurus in his left hand. The dust jacket from Beegee's geography book fit it almost perfectly.

Just below the broad plaza in front of the museum was the entrance to the park, marked by two stone pillars. Fuzzle pumped toward them on his new skateboard, the one he'd bought with all his birthday and allowance money. He looked down at his feet, pleased.

The new board was over two feet long, a flexible, fiberglass kicktail with extrawide trucks. The trucks were the best part, even though buying them had wiped him out. He knew coil-spring suspension ones would be better, but he couldn't afford them yet. But someday, he promised himself, when he was old enough to babysit and was raking in the money, he'd have a whole collection of boards—wood for speed, fiberglass for tricks—and they'd all have suspension—trucks and super wheels with sealed ball-bearings packed in grease. Then he'd hitchhike to California, where they had special parks and banked tracks just for skateboarding. Someday . . .

Beyond the stone pillars a path wound down a long hill to the Boat Pond. Fuzzle pushed off, pumping quickly from cruise to speed. People either stepped aside to let him pass or he skirted them with a slight shift in weight. The bushes and tree trunks blurred and the distant street noises faded. He felt the wind against his face and sensed the pavement slip away. It was like flying, without the noise of the engines—as if the wheels of his skateboard, like the wheels of an airplane after takeoff, had folded up and he was riding on air, skimming above the ground in an endless, floating glide.

The walk pitched steeply just before it merged with the asphalt path that circled the Boat Pond. Fuzzle braked by dragging the worn toe of his left sneaker. Then, knees bent, he swooped right and then left around the pond. Just before he reached the far end he hung way out, put his right hand on the ground, and pivoted in a full circle. Almost. The board slipped out from under him at the last moment.

It must be the thesaurus, Fuzzle thought, picking himself up. It affected his balance. He wished he could get rid of it, hide it under a bush or behind a tree. A lot of leaves, edged and streaked with yellow, lay on the grass. Maybe he could make a pile of them and bury it.

No. It would take too long. Fuzzle sighed. He pushed his free hand into the pocket of his sweat jacket and took out a new pack of bubble gum. He tore it open and piece by piece stuffed the whole pack into his mouth; then he scrunched up the leftover wrappings and was about to drop them onto the walk when he remembered Jonathan's father. He put them back in his pocket instead.

While he chewed to soften the gum, Fuzzle surveyed the artificial pond. Even now he found it hard to believe that skateboarders were messing about where water had always been. All during the summer people had lain on their stomachs or paced around the edge watching their model boats heel and scud in all directions. But the day before school opened the pond had been drained for cleaning and repairs. Fuzzle still remembered his excitement when he'd breezed over the last pitch and discovered the huge, concrete bowl scrubbed and empty.

There was plenty of after-school action in the pond already. The regulars always got there early: the Cherokee Boys, in their beaded headbands; and Crazy Cat; and the Rampaging Rat. Fuzzle knew them only to nod to. They were much older and, besides, there wasn't time for talking.

With the wad of gum tucked into one cheek, he tipped over the rounded lip of the empty pond and went to work on his carves and slides.

The Cherokee Boys were watching him. Fuzzle shot up the sloping wall and kicked out the jams at the top; the front wheels of his board spun in the air impressively above the rim. Then he cranked a turn and rode back into the bowl. He did it again. And again.

The pond was filling up with kids. After a while it was too crowded for a full-bore attack on his power turns.

The thesaurus was a nuisance. His shoulder ached from holding it at arm's length, but he didn't dare put it down. He might forget it.

Crazy Cat kept wiping out right in front of him.

Fuzzle let his board roll to a stop. He flattened the big wad of gum against his teeth with his tongue.

I'll do jumps instead, he decided finally. Switching the book to his other hand, he sidestepped his board out of the pond and stood looking around.

The park bench by the trash cans had a seat and arms but the back was missing. No one was sitting on it. Perfect, thought Fuzzle. I'll drag it to a clear space. But what with the book and his board he had no hands left. First he dropped the book on the grass; then he picked it up and put his skateboard down; then he picked the board back up and put the book down again. Then he thought of a solution: he put the book and the skateboard on the seat of the bench and hauled everything to the middle of the walk.

That does for that, he thought. But now he had something else to think about. The bench wasn't high, but it wasn't low either, and he needed his arms and hands free for the liftoff. The book was a problem. He was about to risk leaving it on the bench when he had a brilliant idea.

In Geography he'd heard about people who carried everything balanced on their heads—wood, bananas, pots of water, even babies. He'd seen pictures of them doing it. One book would be a snap.

But it wasn't as easy as he'd thought. Unless he held on to it, the thesaurus started to slide as soon as he got his board rolling.

Fuzzle wasn't sure why. Maybe his hair was too

clean. He mussed it up, spitting on his hand first, and then he felt the top of his head until he found the flattest spot, near the front. He tried again, holding his head as still as he could. This time the book stayed in place.

Soon he found he could go quite a distance with his arms outstretched and the book riding along all by itself. He practiced bending and straightening his knees, keeping his back stiff and his chin up. The book fell twice, but he caught it both times, even though he had to bail off his board to do it. Then it stopped falling. Fuzzle did a little board boogie.

"Hey!" said a man's voice. "That's not bad."

Fuzzle wondered if the man was talking about him. He hoped so, but he didn't stop to check. Instead he did a few variations on a nose wheelie, steadying the thesaurus every now and then with his hand.

"Not bad at all," said the same voice. "Can you do anything else?"

A woman passed him pushing a double stroller full of babies. Who's he talking to? he wondered.

"You, with the book on your head," said the voice. The woman's head was wrapped in a scarf or a dish towel—Fuzzle wasn't sure which. He must mean me, Fuzzle thought, letting his board roll to a stop. He turned around carefully, keeping his head level. A young man in a brown turtleneck sweater stood on the edge of the grass. Two cameras, one out of its case, hung from his neck on leather straps.

He beckoned to Fuzzle. "Come here a minute, would you?" When Fuzzle pushed over to him he asked again, "Know any other tricks?"

In a whirl all the tricks Fuzzle had learned passed through his mind and disappeared without a trace. The man was eyeing him intently, the way the math teacher did at school when he was waiting for Fuzzle to say something, anything. Fuzzle's mouth opened and closed.

"What were you planning to do with the broken bench?" asked the man after a silence.

The bench. He'd forgotten all about it. "Jump it," said Fuzzle.

"Great! Would you do it for me?"

"I guess so." Fuzzle bent his head and the thesaurus dropped into his hands. The man had a nice face, he decided, and it would only be for a moment. He held out the book. "Watch this for me, will you?"

"I thought you did everything with that on your head." The man's voice sounded disappointed. He didn't reach for the book, so Fuzzle took it back.

"I do, I guess," said Fuzzle. "At least today."

"Good. Just the kind of shot I'm after. Something different."

"Are you going to take my picture?"

"That's the general idea. I'm a reporter for the *West Side Chronicle.* Wouldn't you like to see yourself in print?"

In print, thought Fuzzle. His picture in a real newspaper! Who wouldn't want that? Nobody he knew, except for Jonathan's father, had ever had their picture in a newspaper. Not even Willie or Thelma. Maybe it would be in color, like some of the pictures in his skateboarding magazines. Maybe he'd be in a skateboarding magazine next. And after that . . . Fuzzle stopped imagining. He remembered that he'd never jumped anything with a book on his head before.

"Sure," he said. "It's just that. . ."

"Just what?"

"Nothing," said Fuzzle, "except I'd better practice."

"I can wait," said the reporter cheerfully. "Give a holler when you're ready. I'll set up in front so I can get you head on."

The reporter walked away. Fuzzle put the book back on his head. He was beginning to feel strange without it, as if it had always been there, like his cowlick.

It'll work, he thought, but to make sure, he bent his knees and did an experimental jump off the ground. He felt the weight lift off his head and then a whomp on his left shoulder and a crash. The book lay sprawled on the pavement, half out of its fake jacket, pages rumpled.

Something had gone wrong. Fuzzle wasn't sure what. He checked to see if the reporter was watching, but he was on the far side of the bench bent over his camera, shielding the lens from the sun with his hand. Maybe the glossy geography book jacket was the problem. Fuzzle peeled it off and almost threw it away. Then he remembered it was Beegee's and stuffed it down the neck of his sweat suit.

He tried again. This time the book whacked him on the back before it hit the ground. Why won't it stay on? The reporter wouldn't take his picture without it. I need some glue, that's what I need, Fuzzle thought, shifting the wad of gum to the other side of his mouth. Adhesive tape. . . paste. . . rubber cement. . . He stopped chewing and rolled the gum into a ball with his tongue.

The reporter was squatting on one knee, screwing something onto his camera. His head was down. In a flash Fuzzle had the shiny pink lump out of his mouth and stuck to the front of the thesaurus. He spread it with his fingers until it formed a thick, rubbery circle as big as the palm of his hand. He peeled off his sweat-suit top and set it aside along with Beegee's book jacket. Then he centered the book, gummed side down, on the flat part of his head and pressed. He felt the gum squash and a moist stickiness. Let it dry, he told himself.

The reporter was looking his way now. Fuzzle smiled

and waved. The reporter gave a thumbs-up sign. Fuzzle nodded. The thesaurus didn't move. Fuzzle tried a cautious practice jump. He felt a slight tug, as if someone were pulling his hair, but the book stayed in place.

"I'm ready," he hollered.

He pumped well back to give himself running room and positioned his board carefully, aimed at the middle of the bench. He saw the reporter crouch and raise his camera.

Here goes, thought Fuzzle. He took a deep breath and revved forward with a few quick pumps of his left foot. The bench seemed to come at him with a rush. Fuzzle crouched and waited. At the last moment he leaped, using his knees and arms as launchers.

It was all over in a second. He saw his board flash under the bench and then he was down, landing square and true, as if the board had waited for him on the other side. Arms out, he steadied himself and then pirouetted to a stop in front of the reporter. The book had tilted forward but it was still on his head. Fuzzle reached up to make sure.

"Fantastic!" said the reporter, getting to his feet. Fuzzle caught a glimpse of himself reflected in the dark lens of the camera. "I've never seen anything to beat that. How old are you anyway?"

"Eleven," said Fuzzle.

The reporter whistled through his teeth. "It'll make a great story." He took a spiral pad and a pencil out of his pocket. "I'll need your name."

Fuzzle told him "Francis" at first and then changed his mind. Only Mrs. Dillworth called him "Francis," and "Fuzzle" was a better name for a skateboarder. The reporter wanted to know where he went to school and how long he'd been skateboarding. He was taking notes all the time.

"And what do you call your trick?" he asked finally,

pencil poised. Fuzzle wasn't prepared for that. He'd thought doing it was enough. "'The Book End'?" suggested the reporter. "No good, huh? Never mind. I'll think of something." He flipped his notebook shut.

"Wait," said Fuzzle. "I know." A name had parachuted into his mind. It was just there all of a sudden. "I call it 'The Hot Thesaurus.'"

The reporter opened his notebook again and wrote it down.

"The Hot what?" he asked.

"Thesaurus," said Fuzzle. "Are you going to write about me too?"

"You bet. And don't forget. The *West Side Chronicle*. You'll be in Monday's edition."

"I won't forget." No way, Fuzzle thought. "And thanks a lot."

"Don't thank me," said the reporter. "I should thank you. You're some kind of kid, you know that?" He gave Fuzzle a cuff on the arm.

"Where is everybody?"

"Hi, Fuzzle." His father sat at the kitchen table snapping the ends off string beans and dropping the trimmed beans into a bowl. "I'm here and you're here. That's two. Your mother's at the basketball game—or is it hockey? Anyway, she took all the rest."

Fuzzle ate a raw string bean out of the bowl. "What's for supper?"

"Chicken wings. I'm sitting on them now.

"That doesn't cook them, does it?" asked Fuzzle.

"Defrosts them, I hope. I forgot to take them out of the freezer. But I think it's working. They're softer already. By the way, there's a book on your head. Are you planning to wear it for the rest of the day?"

Fuzzle thought about it. "I'm not sure," he said finally. "Actually, I may have to. But I'm hoping that it will dry up and crumble away. Later. Maybe by bedtime."

"The book?" His father shifted in his chair and felt the seat of his pants. "It's definitely working," he added thoughtfully.

"No. The gum. Underneath." Fuzzle lifted the book with both hands just a little and winced.

"I see," said his father. "A sticky problem, but not insurmountable. Remind me to ask you how you got into this mess. At the moment, however, there are two solutions. Gum disintegrates when frozen." He looked from Fuzzle to the freezer. "But peanut butter works just as well. Here." His father stood up and turned the package of chicken wings over. "You sit on these. I'll get the scissors. We have to separate you from the book first."

The dust jacket of Beegee's geography book crackled inside the top of his sweat suit when Fuzzle sat down. That's another thing I have to remember, he thought.

"Now, raise the book as high as you can." His father waved the scissors like a baton.

Fuzzle lifted and his father snipped. I wonder what scalping feels like, Fuzzle was thinking, when suddenly his head felt light and free.

"Done," said his father triumphantly.

Fuzzle inspected the thesaurus. "Neat," he said. "There isn't that much gum on it." Then he felt his head. The whole front of it was matted and odd—prickly and smooth at the same time. He couldn't imagine what he looked like.

"Do I look okay?" he asked.

"Not okay, but better," said his father. "Still, I think I'm going to get the peanut butter. By the way, how are the wings doing?"

"Melting," said Fuzzle.

"Good." His father opened the cabinet next to the sink. "We've only got chunky, but unless I miscalculate, the lumps should wash out." He unscrewed the top of the jar and scooped out a huge gob with his hand.

Fuzzle felt a heavy splat on the top of his head and his father's fingers beginning to knead and massage. He sniffed. The kitchen smelled like a giant sandwich. His father stepped back holding his hands away from his sides. He looked as if he were wearing peanut-butter gloves.

"Is this one of your inventions? Like the combination razor and comb?" asked Fuzzle. He turned his eyes up, trying to see his hair. People hadn't thought the Raz-or-Comb was so great.

"I'm not sure who thought of this first," said his father, "but I'm glad I didn't go to the game. I'm having more fun here." He went back to his picking and rubbing.

"I think the chicken wings are done," said Fuzzle after a while.

"So are you," said his father. "You can wash your hair now. The gum will come out with the peanut butter. I would advise you, however, not to put the book back on your head."

"You're right—it's still got a lot of gum on it," Fuzzle said, pointing to the cover.

"Leave it here. I'll fix it."

"With peanut butter?" Fuzzle touched the place on his head where the gum had been. His hair was a mass of spikes, gooey and full of what felt like gravel.

"No." His father turned on the hot water with his elbow and began to rinse his hands. "It would stain. I'll do it the other way."

Fuzzle was almost out of the kitchen when he remembered. "I forgot to tell you," he called back. "I'm going to be in the newspaper on Monday."

• •

"And that's me!" said Fuzzle, pointing with his nose. He'd spread the newspaper open and was holding it flat against the wall of the cleaning closet with both hands.

Willie looked at the picture. It was very large— three columns wide and sharp, with a lot of lines of text underneath it.

"I'll show you my name," said Fuzzle. "Somebody hold this corner. Thanks, Thelma. See? There it is, right there."

Beegee climbed up on a bucket to get a better look.

"Get down," said Amanda. "You're blocking my view."

"I wish I could do something terrific like that," sighed Henry wistfully.

"It's a great action shot," said Willie. All sorts of people, people Fuzzle had never met—important people—were probably looking at it right at that very moment. Willie wondered how that made Fuzzle feel. It wouldn't bother me, he thought.

Fuzzle ran his finger under the words as he read. *". . . an eleven-ear-old radical skateboarder, inventor of freestyling's latest twist, 'The Hot Thesaurus.'"*

"The what?" said Thelma, letting go of her end of the paper. The pages curled off the wall like a slow-motion wave.

"'The Hot Thesaurus.' Didn't you see it on my head?"

"Oh my God!" said Thelma. "We're blown!" She stared at Willie.

"Hold on," said Willie. "Maybe she doesn't get the *West Side Chronicle*."

"Who's 'she'?" asked Grace.

"Dogged Dillworth. Who else?" Thelma told her. "Dillworth? What's she got to do. . ." Jonathan's voice trailed away. Amanda gasped.

"Mrs. Dillworth?" said Fuzzle from under the drooping newspaper.

"Oh, dear," cried Amanda. "I knew, I just knew we'd never get away with it. Not in a million years."

"Stop blubbering," said Thelma. "She hasn't caught us yet."

"We'd better hide the evidence, though, in case she does," said Jonathan.

"Right. Gimme the book, Fuzz," ordered Willie.

Fuzzle didn't turn around. With his back to the group he was slowly folding up the newspaper, first in half, then in quarters. He'd reduced it to the size of a comic book, but he kept on folding.

"You mean the thesaurus?" he asked, speaking to the wall.

"The Hot Thesaurus," said Willie. "Hand it over."

"Can't. Don't have it." The newspaper was the size of an address book and Fuzzle was trying to wedge it into his pocket. The collar of his jacket muffled his words.

"What? I can't hear you." Thelma pulled at Fuzzle's shoulder.

"I mean, uh, I don't have it with me," said Fuzzle, louder.

"Fantastic! It's not on you then," said Willie. "Where'd you leave it?"

Fuzzle swung part way around. "Ah—at home. Yes, I left it at home."

"Great." Willie paused. Fuzzle had a funny look on his face. "Where at home?"

"Well, that's the thing of it, sort of. I can't remember the exact place," said Fuzzle. He stared at the plastic clothespins on the line.

"You've got to be kidding," said Thelma.

"He's lost it," said Grace, "and we're in the you-know-what."

"I warned you," said Willie.

"I haven't lost it. I'm positive I haven't lost it. I just don't know exactly where it is at this very moment. But it's somewhere. I'm sure it's somewhere."

"Where? Think!" said Willie.

"I am. Give me a minute."

A minute, an hour, a century. What difference would it make, thought Willie, staring at Fuzzle in despair. But Thelma was nodding her head and smiling.

"That's the way, Fuzzle. Take your time," she said encouragingly. "Here's a bucket. Sit down. Relax. Got a piece of candy, Henry? Good. Okay, now. Go back, Fuzzle. Try to remember everything you did Friday from the moment you left school. Don't hurry. There's no rush." Thelma folded her arms across her chest and gave Willie a warning glance. Fuzzle sat on the bucket, his brow furrowed. He began to tick off his fingers one by one.

"The friendly bit. Always works," Thelma said to Willie out of the corner of her mouth.

"Where are you now?" she asked, when Fuzzle started on his other hand.

"Still in the park, jumping," Fuzzle told her. A little later he murmured "chicken wings," and after that "peanut butter," and then: ". . . stain . . . freeze it . . . freezer! That's it!" He raised his head and beamed at Thelma. "It's in the freezer!"

"In the freezer?" said Henry. "How long has it been there?"

"Not long," said Fuzzle. "Only since Friday."

"It sure isn't 'The Hot Thesaurus' anymore," said Willie.

"Frozen solid, I bet," said Henry. "We'd better get it out."

"At least it's safe," said Thelma. "Dillworth would never think of looking there."

"But Mrs. Dillworth doesn't need to look *any*where anymore. All she needs is the picture. Can't you understand? That *proves* Fuzzle has it—and we're his friends," said Amanda.

Willie let the thought sink in. "I guess she could always sweat the freezer part out of us," he said at last.

"I wonder what's the worst she can do to us for stealing a book," said Beegee.

"If she lays a finger on me," said Amanda, "my father will sue."

"We can worry about that if we have to," said Willie. "Right now we've got to clear out of here, go to class, and act as if nothing has happened. If anyone runs into Dillworth, smile. Don't flinch or look guilty. And don't stick together. If you're hauled in for questioning, hold out as long as you can. We'll figure out the rest later." He opened the door. "Quick! But one at a time."

They went down the stairs single file with big spaces between them—Henry in front, Willie six steps behind, and the rest following. Nothing happened until they reached the fourth floor. Then Willie saw Henry stop and stiffen.

"What's wrong," he whispered, closing the gap between them.

"Oh, geez," said Henry. "Look!"

"Where?" asked Willie impatiently. They were all bunched in a group. It made him nervous.

"There," said Henry, pointing.

Fuzzle's picture, with the caption and everything, was pinned to the bulletin board right outside their classroom door.

"Get rid of it," said Thelma. "Quick!"

Willie was already in motion. He ripped the clipping off the board and crumpled it up, leaving a corner of newspaper still under the pin.

"That was close," said Jonathan.

"I hope Dillworth didn't see it," said Grace. "I hope nobody did."

"Somebody has or it wouldn't have been there," Willie told her.

"And that's only one copy," whispered Amanda. "There must be hundreds and thousands more!"

9

"AMANDA'S NOT EXAGGERATING, for once," said Thelma.

"I tell you, it's a real crisis," said Amanda as she pulled out the pin that had anchored Fuzzle's picture to the bulletin board. The torn bit of newspaper fluttered to the floor. "Thesauruses aren't cheap, you know," she added, jabbing at the cork.

"She'll get us for grand larceny," muttered Thelma darkly.

"I guess it's all my fault," said Fuzzle.

"Shut up. I've got to think," said Willie. "I'm really sorry," said Fuzzle.

"Okay, okay," said Willie, "just let me think."

"Never mind, Fuz," said Beegee. "At least you didn't lose it."

"Besides, you're a celebrity. You're famous. She wouldn't *dare* do anything to you," Jonathan told him.

"Okay, here's the plan," Willie said. "It's an emergency, right? We take emergency measures."

"What?" asked Fuzzle.

"Don't ask questions. Listen," said Willie. "First, leave 'it' right where it is. Got that, Fuz?"

"Got it," said Fuzzle, nodding furiously.

"The rest of you, keep your eyes open all week. Watch the bulletin boards for more pictures. Watch the library. Watch Dillworth—that's the most important. Who she sees, where she goes. Check the teachers' mailboxes in the lobby for any suspicious notes."

"Hey! What if I write *Found* in teacher-type script on Mrs. Dillworth's lost notice? That might throw her off the track," offered Beegee.

"Good thinking," said Willie.

"And right after school I will go to every newsstand in the whole city if I have to and buy up every single copy of the *West Side Chronicle*," said Amanda.

"Won't that cost a fortune?" asked Grace. "Where are you going to get that much money so quickly?"

"I—" Amanda bent and released both snaps on her schoolbag—"always"—she rummaged through the three compartments— "carry cash on me" —she waved a dark red leather purse with a tiny zipper over her head—"for emergencies."

"Great!" said Willie. "Do it then. Also, everybody lie low—you know, blend in. Don't do anything noticeable. That means you've got to pay attention in class and do your homework. Fuzzle? You listening? Don't bust a gut. We'll help you. Right?"

Everyone nodded. "But don't be too super. Better make a few mistakes or they'll really think something's up," warned Thelma.

"If you have something to report, tell me directly. I don't want anything written down. And one more thing: no meetings. Pretend you don't know the closet exists." Willie looked around the group to make sure they understood. "If everything goes all right, we can start our meetings again next week. Who hasn't had the book? Oh, yes, Henry. You're next, but wait till I give you the go ahead."

Early the following day Willie found out from Fuzzle that the thesaurus was still in the freezer, clammy but otherwise fine. Amanda reported exactly how much seventy-three copies of the *West Side Chronicle* had cost and added that she'd given them to Grace's mother, who was extremely grateful for the extra newspaper.

During recess Grace and Jonathan helped Fuzzle get a start on the back papers in the bottom of his locker and Willie and Thelma worked ahead in their reading-skills workbooks.

"Nothing to it," said Thelma. "I'm on page one hundred and two already."

Thelma was way ahead of him, so Willie decided to take his book home and do a couple of sections every night.

That afternoon several kids asked Fuzzle if he was the Fuzzle in the newspaper. Fuzzle told Willie that he'd said no, there were lots of Fuzzles around who looked just like him.

Before the 8:20 bell on Wednesday, Beegee found Willie in the gym practicing foul shots. When Willie heard what Beegee had to say, he stopped shooting and stood still, bouncing the basketball every now and then as he listened. Beegee told him that on his way through the lobby he had seen the librarian and Mrs. Dillworth disappearing into the principal's office.

"So I asked the nurse what was up," Beegee reported, "and she said there was a problem in the library. So I said, 'What problem?' And she said something about how it had been going on too long and now they were forced to deal with it. What did she mean, Willie?"

"Just what she said, I guess." Willie held the basketball in both hands. "And I don't like it a whole lot."

On Thursday Amanda turned in a book report for extra credit. She told Willie about it on the way to math class. "I left a copy on Mrs. Dillworth's card table," she said, "with a nice note and illustrations."

"Anyone in your house getting suspicious, Fuzzle?" Willie asked when the class was over. "I mean, a book in the freezer and all."

"I don't think so. My father just moves it around in there." Fuzzle thought for a moment. "I'm not sure he notices. It looks sort of like another package of frozen potpies."

Three things happened on Friday:

First, Jonathan and Grace reported that Fuzzle, with their help, had finished most of his missing assignments and corrections. The bottom of his locker was almost bare.

Second, Mrs. Dillworth's Lost and Found notice disappeared from the cluttered bulletin board, leaving a brown square of cork where it had been. "It's eerie," Amanda said to Willie. "Worse than the notice." The empty space made them all uneasy. To fill up the hole Willie tacked up an unsigned drawing of a basketball player dribbling downcourt.

And third, a second-grader threw up on the floor at lunch.

"Must have been something she ate for breakfast," said Mrs. Cleft, loud enough for the whole lunchroom to hear. Willie wanted to splat her with his piece of olive loaf.

"Calm down," said Henry. "Eat your cole slaw."

"This isn't cole slaw," said Willie. "It's mayonnaise soup. I can't grow on this revolting stuff. I have no stamina anymore. When I play basketball my hands sweat. I can't drive or rebound or anything."

"You can jump a lot higher than I can," said Henry.

"I've gotta do *something*," Willie muttered to himself, "before I'm stunted for life."

"Well, I'm nervous—I can't eat anything anyway," said Amanda. "Remember special-reading class? It's next." Willie had remembered it off and on all morning.

For once, Fuzzle got there on time, but Mrs. Dillworth didn't give him more than a quick glance.

"Work on sight recognition. No word-card drill today," she said curtly. After that she paid almost no attention to them at all. She spent most of the period writing page after page on a lined pad. Willie kept his voice low anyway, when he made his discovery about the table.

"My knees don't fit under anymore," he said.

"They never did," whispered Thelma. "Sit sideways."

"She's watching us," hissed Grace. "I can feel it." Willie checked. She was.

"Keep your nose in your book and don't look at the big shelves," said Thelma.

"Can you see if my book report is still on her table?" Amanda asked Willie. "I put it in a green folder." Willie shook his head.

On his way out of the library, Henry stopped at Mrs. Dillworth's table. "Good-bye," he said, smiling. "It was a pretty good class."

"I'm glad you enjoyed it," said Mrs. Dillworth. She didn't smile back.

"Henry," said Willie later. "Look, leave that stuff to Amanda."

• •

Nothing else happened before the weekend. And Monday was normal. Nobody stopped them. Nobody questioned them. Willie let Tuesday go by just to make sure. On Wednesday morning he gave the all clear.

"We're safe," he announced. "Out of danger. Cancel the emergency measures. Henry, you can pick up the book at Fuzzle's and we'll meet in the closet as usual tomorrow."

"Sure you don't want it first?" Henry asked him.

"Don't worry about me," said Willie. "My turn will come, and when it does, I'm going to blow this place wide open."

10

HENRY ATE a whole quart of butter-pecan ice cream at Fuzzle's. He didn't mean to, but it worked out that way.

When Fuzzle opened the freezer, they found the thesaurus buried under a lot of other stuff. Henry took the ice cream out just to be helpful. Then Fuzzle went to work scraping the gum off the front of the book with a knife. It was hard as a rock and came off easily in little chips.

To keep Fuzzle company, Henry got a spoon and sat down at the kitchen table. He didn't want to bother Fuzzle by asking for a bowl, so he ate right out of the carton. When he'd finished half the quart, he decided he ought to stop, after a few more bites, but then there was so little left that it didn't seem worthwhile putting it back in the freezer. There was nothing more annoying, Henry knew, than finding out that what you thought was a full quart of ice cream was actually almost empty.

Later, boarding the bus, Henry felt so full that he almost wished that he hadn't had to finish it off. There was an empty seat by the door and Henry sat down gratefully, after checking to see if there were any older people who wanted it. He leaned forward to settle his shopping bag between his knees. It was then he heard a funny sound behind him—a ripping, zipping sound. At the same time he felt something like a very fast, light-footed bug run up the back seam of his pants. He stayed bent over, studying the contents of his bag intently while he reached one hand around in back to check.

Split. His pants. From crotch to belt. A long, gaping hole.

How am I going to get home, Henry thought in a panic. I'll have to stay on this bus until dark.

But by the time the bus reached his corner there were a lot of people standing in the aisle and Henry decided he could sidle out without anyone noticing. Once he was on the street, though, it was a different matter. There was nothing to hide behind.

Henry squeezed his bottom and his legs together as tight as he could, praying that the big squeeze would help hold the material closed. Then he inched along the pavement, taking tiny steps, staying as close to the shop walls as he could.

Grocery store, hardware store, fruit stand, art gallery. It was murder. Now I know how a worm feels, he thought. At the hairdresser's he stopped to rest under the scalloped awning, his back against the glass. Then he moved slightly away and, turning only the upper part of his body, tried to catch a glimpse of his back reflected in the window.

His underpants were showing. No doubt about it. Against the blue of his corduroys, the white was like a beacon. Inside the hairdresser's a lady stared out at him from under a pink metal hair dryer. Her lips curled up. It wasn't a smile. It was a smirk. Definitely a smirk, thought Henry. She's seen my underpants. She knows.

He felt a hotness spread through his body, up to his head and out to his hands. Everybody can see them, Henry thought.

Suddenly, he stripped off his turtleneck sweater and tied it low around his waist, leaving him naked from the belt up. Goose pimples popped out all over his bare skin and passersby gave him questioning looks, but Henry was so relieved he hardly felt the cold. Better for people to think he was crazy or a health nut or anything than to see his *underwear*.

When he got home, the smell of cookies baking beckoned to him, but he ignored it. His mother and grandmother were busy in the kitchen, so he made it to his room without being seen. Henry took off all of his clothes except for his underpants and stuffed his ripped corduroys under the wadded papers in his wastebasket. He never wanted to see them again. They were too small anyway. Then he took his blue terry-cloth bathrobe off the hook in the bathroom and threw it around his shoulders. He caught a glimpse of himself in the full-length mirror on the back of the bathroom door and stopped. A prizefighter. That's kind of what I look like, he thought. That was the way they wore their satin bathrobes. Maybe he ought to ask for a red satin bathrobe for Christmas.

Henry began to prance and bob on the balls of his feet, his arms bent, fists clenched, dodging, jabbing, attacking. All the time he watched himself in the mirror. When the bathrobe slid off his shoulders, he put his arms through the sleeves and belted it loosely, so it was open down the front. I guess I look more like one of those terrific Japanese wrestlers, he thought, or a weight lifter. Bet I could lift a thousand pounds if I wanted to.

He could see himself in the Olympics up against the Russians. Bending his knees, he got a good grip on an imaginary barbell and with a mighty jerk lifted it chest high. He checked his stance in the mirror. His muscles bulged, his legs could hardly stand the strain, but there was nowhere to go but up. Grunting fiercely, he planted his feet and steeled himself for a final effort. In one smooth movement he raised the barbell past his shoulders, past his head, and locked his elbows in place. The crowd roared, but Henry stood like a rock, his eyes fixed on the judges' box. Would they ever make up their minds?

"Good heavens, Henry. What are you doing?"

The barbell dropped with a crash.

"Nothing," said Henry.

"Why are you here in the bathroom in your bathrobe?" asked his mother. "Aren't you feeling well?"

"I've got a lot of homework," mumbled Henry, brushing past her.

"Well, you start then," said his mother. "I'll bring you a snack. What about some homemade chocolate chip cookies? They're just out of the oven."

"Okay," said Henry, unloading his shopping bag onto his desk. When his mother came back, he was writing busily, so she set the tall glass of milk and the plate piled high with cookies by his elbow and left without disturbing him.

As soon as she was gone, Henry dropped his pencil, chucked down a cookie, and went back to the mirror. He crouched in front of it like a wrestler, swaying from side to side with outstretched arms, waiting for

an opening. He clenched his teeth and drew his lips back in a sneer. But it wasn't any good. His opponent in the mirror was still a barefoot fat boy wearing a blue bathrobe.

"I'm fat," said Henry out loud. He felt like a nincompoop talking to himself in front of a mirror, and he didn't like the sound of the word *fat* either. It sounded like something he didn't want to be. Maybe there was a better word to describe himself, not quite so short and, well, thudding. A nicer word.

Overweight was the only other word he could think of, but that was the kind of word that doctors wrote on charts. His doctor had been writing it on Henry's chart for years—so often in fact that Henry had stopped wondering or even caring whether he was more overweight than the time before or how much over his weight he actually was. There must be another word for me, thought Henry—and then he remembered the thesaurus. "Why not?" he said to himself. "I lugged it all the way home."

It took him a while to find the right page, but when he did he discovered that *fat* was followed by a whole string of other words, beginning with *big, great, massive,* and *mighty.* Not bad, thought Henry, reaching for another cookie. Not bad at all. He drank half his milk and got out a clean piece of paper. I think I'll write them down. Crumbs fell on the page, but Henry didn't notice.

At the dinner table Henry's father noticed that Henry wasn't eating. Henry's plate was piled high with ham and lima beans and sweet potatoes topped with a marshmallow crust, but he was just poking about with his fork.

"Eat up," said Henry's father, "before it gets cold."

"I'm not hungry," said Henry.

"Of course you are," said his grandmother. "You're a growing boy and all growing boys are hungry."

"I'm grown," Henry told her.

"Are you feeling all right?" asked his mother in a worried voice. "You didn't look too well this afternoon."

"I don't look too well, ever." Henry stabbed his fork into his sweet potatoes.

"Whatever are you talking about, Henry?" asked his grandmother.

"I'm talking about being lumpish and puffy and. . . and obese," said Henry to his lima beans. "I'm talking about being. . . elephantine!"

"For heaven's sake, Henry. There's nothing wrong with being a lusty, ah—strapping boy," said his father.

"Or well fed," added his mother.

"You look lovely, dear," said his grandmother. She reached over and patted his cheek. "Plump as a dumpling."

"I am not plump as a dumpling!" shouted Henry. "I'm fat as a pig! Anyone can see that!"

Henry's family stared at him in silence. Henry turned to his mother. "Look," he said. "I wouldn't mind if I were just large. . . or stalwart. . . or full-grown or even bulky. But I'm not. Just look at me. I'm fleshy and lubberly and bulbous. I'm the last one up the stairs and I don't like to go swimming because I look like a blimp in a bathing suit. I even split my pants on the bus today."

"Your pants? You did?" Henry's father looked down at Henry's pants.

"Not these—I threw them out."

"Maybe they were too tight," suggested his grandmother.

"They were, but it's not their fault. They were pretty new. I got too fat for them and they busted."

"Your mother will get you another pair," said his father. "Don't think about them anymore.

"I'm thinking about me. I'm thinking that maybe I shouldn't eat anymore," said Henry.

"Starving," said his grandmother seriously, "is very, very unhealthy."

"He won't starve," said Henry's mother, pushing her plate away. "But you know, you're right, Henry. You could stand to lose a few pounds. So could I, for that matter." She ran her hands over her hips. "We'll start a family diet tomorrow. Okay, Henry? Just eat your meat and beans tonight." Henry nodded.

"Well," said his grandmother, "he may be a trifle overweight, but if you want my opinion—and no one ever does—bulbous he is not!"

Henry was a block and a half ahead, but Willie spotted him immediately, even from a distance—even from behind. Especially from behind, thought Willie. But there was something different about Henry that morning. It took Willie a moment to figure out what: Henry was carrying three shopping bags instead of one. He was walking slower than usual, too, sort of dragging along. Willie jogged to catch up.

"What've you got there, Hen?" he asked.

Henry stopped and put the bags down on the sidewalk. There were red lines across the palms of his hands where the string handles had cut into the skin. He rubbed his hands against his pants. "Food," he said. Willie peered into the bags. Henry wasn't kidding.

It looked like he'd cleaned out a delicatessen.

"Why are you bringing it to school?" he asked.

Henry picked up the bags again and trudged forward. Other people on the street were carrying briefcases and hurrying. "I don't want it anymore, but it's too good to waste. So I thought we could have a party— you know, at the meeting. Sort of a welcome-back party." Henry paused and then he began to walk a little faster. He didn't look at Willie. "Actually," he said, "more of a farewell party. To my snacks and candy. I've decided to go on a diet."

Willie walked along beside him. He thought of saying something polite—like: Why? You're not *that* fat. Or: Gee, Henry, that's super! Which was closer to the truth, but he didn't want to sound too enthusiastic. Henry might take it the wrong way. He wished he could come up with something in between.

"I brought the thesaurus," Henry said. "It's at the bottom of the bag with the pretzels on top."

"Good." Willie was still thinking about Henry's diet. "Hey," he said suddenly. "You know what, Henry? You're a lifesaver!"

"You want one?" asked Henry. "I have a whole pack."

"I mean your idea about a party. It'll save me from lunch."

"Lunch?" said Henry. "I wonder what's for lunch?. . ."

"Since it's Thursday, it's gotta be chicken al la king. With acne. Little red bits—for color, you know." Willie grabbed his throat and let his tongue loll out of his mouth.

"Pimentos?"

"That's what Cleft calls them, but I have my doubts. It doesn't matter now anyway. We can stuff ourselves in the cleaning closet, thanks to you. We'll pass the word to the others when we get to school. Here, let me carry one of those. They must weigh a ton."

Willie bounded up the stairs at recess. Henry had added all the snacks he'd stored in his locker to the stuff he'd brought from home, and Grace had washed out an almost empty poster-paint jar and had filled it with water from a drinking fountain. Beegee and Jonathan and Fuzzle were each lugging a shopping bag so Henry could get up the stairs faster. When they reached the cleaning closet, Willie looked quickly up and down the hall to see if anyone else was watching and then grinned at Thelma and opened the door.

Dillworth! Willie's smile fled. His breath was sucked down his throat. Dillworth in a chair behind a desk, leering at him! Willie froze in his tracks but the others were crowding in after him. He was shoved halfway into the room before the scuffling and giggling behind him faded and died.

It's a trick! he thought wildly. Or a mistake! Maybe it's the wrong floor—maybe this isn't our closet. Two chairs he had never seen before, each with a broad paddle-shaped arm, were lined along one wall, and in a pot on the floor in front of him there was a large plant with sharp, spiky leaves. Maybe I'm dreaming, thought Willie. He took a slow, cautious step backward and then another. He stepped on someone's foot.

"Don't go, Willie," said Mrs. Dillworth. "I want to talk to you. You too, Thelma. And Amanda. Is she here by any chance?"

Willie didn't answer. He was sure this was the right floor and he knew this was really their cleaning closet, even though the pails and mops were gone. So was the clothesline. And the sinks—they were gone, too. How do you take sinks out without causing a flood? Willie wondered.

Dillworth was coming toward him. The leaves of the plant caught at her skirt; Willie turned sideways to get out of her way. She pushed past to the others bunched behind him.

"The rest of you can go on about your business," she said. "I have a small matter to discuss with your friends." She made a bridge with her hand high on the doorframe and pushed them along with her other arm. Out they went, one by one, stunned. Jonathan trailed his shopping bag full of Henry's snacks along the floor and disappeared out the door after Beegee and Fuzzle. Grace, still clutching the water jar against her chest, turned to give Willie a last look. "Hurry along now," said Mrs. Dillworth. Henry squeezed by her and then Mrs. Dillworth closed the door.

11

HANG IN THERE, thought Willie. He stared at a poster taped to the wall behind Mrs. Dillworth's desk. It showed a huge eye connected by veiny red and blue lines to a blob labeled BRAIN. The blob was pinkish gray and lumpy, like piled fat worms. I can't look there, he decided, and he turned toward Amanda instead. At least she hadn't started to whine. Not yet. But she'd never hold out. She'd crack like an egg.

The waxers and vacuum cleaners had been replaced by a row of gray file cabinets. Thelma was leaning against one of them, her feet crossed and her hands on her hips. She gave a slight jerk of her head upward. Willie followed her gaze. The old, bare light bulb had been covered with a pink shade, all frills and sharp folds. Thelma wrinkled her nose ever so slightly. Cool, thought Willie. He was glad she was there.

"Well," said Mrs. Dillworth, rubbing her hands together in a satisfied way. "Isn't this cozy?—like peas in a pod. Just the three of you, and me." She's softening us up, thought Willie. He clamped his jaws shut and faced the chart on the wall. We'll look like that eye before she's through, he thought.

"I like your lampshade, Mrs. Dillworth," said Amanda in a high-pitched voice.

"It adds a bright touch, doesn't it? As a matter of fact, I made it myself." Mrs. Dillworth was back behind her desk now, but she didn't sit down. Willie hadn't remembered her being so tall.

"The whole room has turned out better than I expected," she continued. "Everyone rallied round, as it were, to help a lame dog over a stile. The science teacher lent me that interesting poster, for example, and they even added a ventilating fan so I wouldn't smother. Ha, ha." For the first time Willie became aware of a steady whirring sound. It seemed to fill the room. "It's so nice to be out of the library and into an office of my own, small as it is. But more important, nothing can disturb us here."

"It's really lovely," squeaked Amanda.

"I'll bet you didn't even know this little closet existed," said Mrs. Dillworth.

"It's a surprise all right," said Thelma.

"Why don't you sit down. Make yourselves comfortable," said Mrs. Dillworth. "At least two of you can, that is." Amanda sat, in the chair closest to the door.

"I'd rather stand," said Thelma.

"Me too," said Willie.

"Suit yourselves." Mrs. Dillworth sat down, smoothing her skirt under one hip, and edged her chair closer to the desk. The chair made a harsh scraping sound against the floor. Then she put her elbows on the blotter and lowered her chin onto her clasped hands. There seemed to be too many eyes—Mrs. Dillworth's and the enormous bloodshot eye behind her head. Willie felt a little dizzy.

"Now," said Mrs. Dillworth, "it's time, I think, for us to have our little talk."

Here it comes, thought Willie. He tried to wipe the thesaurus out of his mind completely. I don't know anything, I don't know anything, he practiced saying over and over in his head.

Classes were changing on the lower floors. Willie could hear the sharp bangs of lockers closing and the clamor of feet and voices drifting up the stairwell. A few kids climbed the last flight and headed toward the library, but nobody did more than glance at the three of them huddled in the corner at the top of the stairs.

"I thought I was going to faint," said Amanda, looking back at the door of what had been the cleaning closet.

"From the very beginning, remember, I swore I was going to get out—and now I am!" exclaimed Thelma. "Who would believe that finishing a dumb reading-skills workbook would do it?"

"She absolutely loved my book report on *Charlotte's Web*," said Amanda, "and I didn't even read the book! Zelly and I watched the movie version on TV last week."

"And she didn't even mention the thesaurus," said Thelma.

"Don't tell the others," said Willie suddenly.

"What do you mean don't tell them? Don't tell them weve been promoted? You must be crazy!" said Amanda. She straightened against the wall and stared at him with round eyes. "I'm going to tell Zelly. And my mother. I can't wait. I'll call her long distance, person to person, tonight."

"Why, Willie?" asked Thelma. "Why not tell?"

"Not yet," said Willie. "I don't want them to know—yet. We don't start in E Group until Monday. We can tell them then."

"I don't see any point in putting it off," said Amanda.

"What's the big deal, Willie?" asked Thelma.

"There's Henry's party for starters," Willie told them, "and besides, I need them. For a little while longer. It's my turn with the thesaurus, remember? And there's something I want to do. Something I can't do alone."

"What?" asked Amanda. "I mean, what could be that important?"

"You'll find out," said Willie, "but you have to promise to keep quiet about the promotion thing first."

"They're going to ask why Dillworth wanted to see us. What are we supposed to tell them?" asked Thelma.

"The truth is always the best," said Amanda.

"Not always," said Thelma.

"Let me figure out what to say. You two don't have to say anything. It will be my lie—okay, Amanda?"

"Here comes Beegee," warned Thelma. "And the rest of them."

"Promise, Amanda?" said Willie insistently. "You've got to promise.

"All right. All right. If it means that much to you." Amanda hooked one finger around her gold chain and pressed her lips together in a thin line.

"Are you guys okay?" asked Beegee. He looked them all over as if for welts and scratches. "What happened?"

"We waited for a while outside the door," said Grace.

"But we couldn't hear a word and there wasn't any keyhole. Besides, Jonathan thought we looked suspicious."

"What did she say?" asked Jonathan. "What did she do to you?"

"Nothing," said Willie. "She asked a lot of questions. That's all."

"What kind of questions?" asked Beegee.

"Just questions," said Willie. "But we didn't tell her a thing."

"I knew you wouldn't," said Grace with a triumphant nod of her head. Her eyes were shining at him.

"Amanda was great," said Willie, looking away. "She buttered her up like mad."

"Yeah," said Thelma. "She even admired the lampshade, and it's the yuckiest thing you ever saw.

"Phew!" Henry wiped his forehead with the back of his hand. His face was red and sweaty from running up the stairs. "What a relief. Worrying makes me hungry."

"Are we still going to have the party?" asked Fuzzle. "All the food is squished in Henry's locker. It took three of us to close the door."

"Not now. There's no time," said Willie. "Tomorrow, at breakfast."

"At breakfast!" Amanda sounded as if she were going to explode. "Why breakfast? I always have breakfast with Zelly—on trays."

"Not tomorrow," said Willie. "I have a plan. Don't ask me about it. It isn't done yet. But if it's going to work we've all got to get to school really early. Seven-thirty—sharp! And I'll need supplies. Everyone's got to bring something. Sticks. I need sticks—long ones, old mop-handle type things or whatever you can find. And thumbtacks or nails. And a hammer. Anyone got felt-tipped pens? The broad kind—you know, in different colors?"

"I have a complete set—forty-eight colors," said Amanda.

Figures, thought Willie. That was one good thing about Amanda.

"But where are we going to meet," asked Grace, "now that you know-who is you-know-where?"

Willie considered for a moment. "In the gym," he said. "Behind the bleachers. No one will see us there."

"Good," said Henry. "The food wouldn't last long if we had to eat it in the open and share it with the whole school. Gosh. I just thought of something: I better lug the bags home again. Don't dare leave them overnight. Some of the sixth-graders might open my locker and demolish everything."

"You've still got the book, right?" Willie asked him. Henry nodded.

"Don't forget to give it to me. I need it. It's vital." That covered it all: time, place, supplies, food.

Willie couldn't think of anything he'd left out.

The hall was quiet. Willie knew the doors on the floors below were closed and that classes had begun, but he didn't feel like moving. He felt strangely quiet too, and apart, as if the school had nothing to do with him, with any of them—as if the eight of them could stand there forever, if they wanted to, and it would be all right.

"I think we're late for Math again," said Jonathan.

"Better go," said Thelma.

Willie took his time going downstairs. He swung a leg out over each step, slowly and deliberately, before putting his foot down.

"I didn't tell," Amanda whispered to him from one step behind. She tugged at his shirt. "So now you have to tell me. What's this breakfast-plan thing all about?"

"Signs," said Willie. He swung a leg out. He put a foot down. "It's about signs."

12

IT WAS DARK and eerie under the bleachers—so dark, in fact, that Willie wasn't sure if he was alone or not.

"Hi. Anyone there?" he called softly. No answer. He looked quickly behind him. No one. Funny—he could have sworn someone was watching him. He ducked out from under the bleachers to check the time by the large caged clock on the wall and found that he was ten minutes early. He could see daylight outside the high meshed windows, but the big gym was gray and dim. The basketball hoops floated against the rectangular backboards high above his head—higher than he could ever possibly reach—and the netting hung limp and still. Willie hoped that in ten minutes the light would be stronger. Maybe his eyes were adjusting. It seemed brighter already.

"I can get started," he said to himself. He went back under the bleachers. There was just enough light slanting through the slits between the bleacher seats for him to work by. He laid the five large pieces of poster board flat, side by side against the wall, and opened the thesaurus to the last page he had marked.

Just then he heard the creak of cautious steps on the hard floor; Beegee, a bundle of sticks in one hand, and Fuzzle, carrying a mop, showed up at the far end of the bleachers and peered in. They smiled when they saw Willie.

"Hi," they whispered.

"Hi," said Willie. Something about the size and silence of the gym made him whisper too, as though words, out loud, would echo and echo until ghosts answered back.

Other figures soon appeared, framed by the bleacher supports.

"Don't just stand there," whispered Willie. "C'mon in."

"I'm hungry," said Fuzzle, stooping over and carrying his mop like a lance. "Where's Henry?"

"Watch out!" said Willie. "Don't step on my signs."

"I thought it was another of your lies," said Amanda, "but you really did mean signs. And there's writing on them." She bent over and squinted at the penciled lines. "'*We Hate Lunch*'?" she read. "'*It makes us Gag, Retch, Heave, Wamble, Keck*'?"

"Willie," Grace warned, "you better not let Mrs.Cleft see this. What's it for, anyway?"

"I want Mrs. Cleft to see it. It's *for* Mrs. Cleft," answered Willie. "They're all for her."

"Listen to this one," said Beegee. " '*Food Here Is Sick! Eat It And You Will Get: Green Sickness, Yellow Jaundice, Scarlet Fever, Pinkeye—*' "

"Shh," said Jonathan, "shh. What's that noise?"

Klunck, slide. Klunck, slide.

It was Henry, dragging his shopping bags.

"Sorry I'm late," he said, "but these things are heavier than barbells. I bet I've lost ten pounds already. I'm weak from hunger. I didn't eat hardly anything last night. Anyone want some barbecue chips or—"

"Later," interrupted Willie. "After we're done lettering."

"Lettering? Lettering what?" asked Henry.

"Willie's signs. Wait till you see them," said Thelma. "They're terrific!"

"But can't we letter and eat at the same time? I think it's all getting stale, and this is my last fling," said Henry.

"Okay, Hen," said Willie, "you be in charge of the food. Did you bring the pens, Amanda? Good. Pass them out. Go over all my penciled letters. Make the lines broad. I want the words to stand out so they're easy to read. Like this." He picked up a green marker and knelt down by the sign closest to him.

L-U-N-C-H— Willie turned the letters green.

"Gimme a red," he said to Amanda, "for the exclamation point."

Bars of light striped the floor under the bleachers as he worked.

"Now purple," said Willie. Thelma slapped it into his hand.

F-O-U-G-H! P-A-H! Y-E-C-K! Willie lettered. "See? Do it like this."

"Any one want some Hostess Twinkies? Or Koconut Krunchies?" said Henry, digging into a shopping bag. "Or here, look—Toffee Morsels."

"Me," said Beegee. "Toss me some."

"Me too," said Grace.

For a while the gym was silent except for the squeaking of pens and the crackle of cellophane.

"Willie? Is *unswallowable* a real word?" asked Thelma, sitting back on her heels. "I've lettered it in anyway."

"That's the one I made up," Willie answered, "but it doesn't matter. It's true."

"Now," said Henry, "who wants Devil Dogs, or French Fried Fritters? And I've got a whole six-pack of Coke at the bottom."

"'*Undrinkable, Inedible,*'" muttered Thelma as she colored those words. Then louder, to Henry: "I'll take some of everything."

"Listen, you guys," said Willie, "when you're finished, bring the posters to me. I'll put 'em on these sticks. Geez. Who brought a whole mop?"

"Me," said Fuzzle.

"Why?" asked Willie.

"You said mop handles. You didn't say one word about taking the mop off."

"Okay, okay, forget it," said Willie. "I guess I can use the other end."

"One bag finished. Two to go," said Henry. "Who's for Tootsie Rolls? Bubble gum? Taco corn chips? Licorice strings? Or—" Henry inspected a small red package—"Crispy Almond Delights?"

"I might like that. What is it?" asked Fuzzle, putting his Magic Marker down.

"Umm. It's '*tender young coconut shavings bathed in thick vanilla cream,*'" read Henry from the package, "'*encased in pure milk chocolate and rolled in freshly roasted almond fragments.*'" Henry swallowed. "Could I share it with you, Fuzz?"

"Go ahead."

"Can I add a word to the 'YECK!' sign?" asked Amanda.

"Sure," said Willie. "The thesaurus is right there by my foot."

"I don't need it," said Amanda. "I know it by heart. It's Zelly's favorite."

"Pass the book to me then," said Grace.

The 8:20 bell clanged. In the gym it sounded like a fire alarm.

"We've got to hurry!" said Willie.

"I wish school was always like this. This is the most fun I've had in all the years I've been here," said Jonathan. He took a long swig of Coke. "And it's about to be over."

"Hey," said Grace, "you're acting like this is a good-bye party or something."

"Well, it is. I'm sort of saying good-bye to food," said Henry. "Anyone want pretzels or pink-marshmallow cookies? Everything else is gone."

"And the cleaning closet," said Beegee. "That's gone too."

"But we're still here." Fuzzle smiled.

"For the moment," said Amanda. Willie and Thelma glared at her. "For the moment," she repeated, staring back.

Willie whacked a thumbtack in, hard, with the hammer.

"Hey, Willie," said Grace, "this piece of poster board is blank."

"I know," said Willie. "I didn't have time to do it."

"Can I use it?" asked Grace.

"Sure. But make it quick." Willie pressed in another tack. Thelma and Beegee held the signs in place for him. The others helped Jonathan pick up the bits of cellophane, the cardboard, the crumbs, the paper wrappers, and the empty cans. They stuffed the trash in Henry's shopping bags.

"It's a little messy, but how do you like it?" asked Grace. She held up her sign for Willie to see.

Willie didn't say anything for a moment. Then he started to laugh. "Pass it over. I'll tack it to the mop."

The other four signs were finished. Willie checked each one and then he stacked them one on top of another face down on the gym floor. "Leave them here."

"Now what?" asked Fuzzle.

"Nothing, said Willie, "until lunchtime. Then we come back here and pick them up."

"What happens next?" asked Fuzzle.

"We strike!"

They struck, halfway through lunch period. Willie picked the moment. He held them back outside the cafeteria door, signs down, words to the wall, until the last stragglers had gone through the lunch line and the noise from the lunchroom had built to a peak.

"Ready?" Willie raised his sign. Thelma's went up

right behind him. Grace lifted hers. Amanda stood beside her to help "if absolutely necessary." Jonathan held his stick with both hands and Fuzzle, beaming, waved his sign over his head.

"Turn it around, Fuzz," ordered Willie. "It's backward."

Henry and Beegee had volunteered to bring up the rear. They were the reserves in case any of the others keeled over.

Willie reviewed his team one last time. The ragged line didn't seem very long. Beegee was hidden by Henry so Willie had to imagine that he was still there. He felt a tightening in his stomach. Maybe they wouldn't be able to make enough noise. Maybe no one would get it. Maybe they would end up the laughingstock of the school. Maybe the principal wouldn't think it was funny. Grace stared at Willie. Her shoulders were back and she looked fierce enough to kill.

"Okay," Willie said. "Don't forget Jonathan's slogan. Shout it as loud as you can so everyone hears." He turned away and raised his sign as high as he could reach. Then he dropped his free arm, stiff and straight, the way he'd seen generals do in war movies. "Forward, march!" he yelled, and stepped through the open doorway.

He saw Mrs. Cleft look up from behind her glass-fronted counter and then automatically reach for her ladle. There was no turning back. Willie lifted his poster high again and waved it in her face as he passed.

"We—think—lunches—stink," he shouted. "We—think— lunches—stink!" Other voices joined him the second time around. Thelma and Grace and Jonathan, he figured.

He passed the end of the counter. The double doors into the lunchroom were propped open. A few kids at the tables closest to him stopped chewing and looked up with startled faces. Willie plunged ahead, out into the lunchroom.

"We—think—lunches—stink!" No one else seemed to notice him. His voice was lost in the din of talk and clatter. Willie circled to his left, pumping his sign up and down. "We—think . . ."

Bang—bang, bang-bang—bang! Bang—bang—bang-bang—bang! He glanced back. Henry and Beegee were just rounding the doorway. Each of them had grabbed a plastic tray and they were whanging away on them with metal spoons. But someone else was at the end of their line: it was Mrs. Cleft, bearing down on Beegee from behind, wielding her dripping ladle. Willie marched faster.

People were paying attention now. A hush spread across the lunchroom, louder than any noise. Their voices sounded thin and weak in the strange silence and someone was stumbling over the words. The chant wavered and faltered. Oh no, Willie thought to himself.

"We—think—lunches—stink!" he bellowed at a table of fourth-graders.

"I do too!" one of them yelled back. She held her nose and hit the top of the table with her fork.

Thump—thump—thump-thump—thump! Feet started to pound the floor. Willie almost slowed to a stop.

"Keep going!" Thelma pushed him from behind. *"We—think— lunches—stink!"* she shouted, fanning the air with her sign, like a conductor, to the beat of the words.

"We—think—lunches—stink!" answered a motley chorus of voices.

Willie swung past a table of older kids—sixth grade or seventh. Their ittouths were moving but Willie couldn't distinguish their voices. By this time, he could barely hear himself. "WE—THINK— LUNCHES—

This Food is Bad
INEDIBLE
NONEDIBLE
UNSWALLOWABLE
UNEATABLE
UNDRINKABLE
Lunch!
Fough!
Pah!
YECK!
UGH!
FOH!
PHEW!
Pew!
Burp!
ICKY POO-POO

WE HATE LUNCH!
IT IS
DISLIKED
DISRELISHED
UNPOPULAR
UNLOVED
UNWANTED
IT MAKES US
GAG
RETCH
HEAVE
WAMBLE
KECK
FOOD HERE IS SICK!
EAT IT AND YOU WILL GET:
Green Sickness
Yellow Jaundice
Scarlet Fever
Pinkeye
Acidosis
Halitosis
Stomach Spasms
Gallstones
Softening of the Brain
Hardening of the Arteries

STINK!" The words thundered in his ears. The whole world seemed to have joined them, banging and stomping and yelling the chant.

Right ahead of him was the teachers' table. Willie saw the principal push back his chair and then stop, his hands still cupped around the edge of the table. Mrs. Dillworth was staring over his head. Willie swung his sign back and forth and Mrs. Dillworth's head swayed with it. The nurse was wiping her eyes with a napkin. The principal let go of the table and hid his mouth with one hand, but his cheeks and eyes gave him away. He's smiling, thought Willie.

It was bedlam. Willie had never heard so much noise in his life. He risked another look back. Amanda was carrying Grace's sign now—mop and all—and she was actually waving it. Fuzzle was parading so hard his knees almost hit his chin.

Willie stopped yelling and just marched in time with the roar of voices. As he turned the last corner, he began to wonder what to do next, whether to go around again or disappear out the far door.

He never had a chance to figure it out. Someone grabbed him from behind. For a moment he thought it must be Mrs. Cleft and he ducked in case she was about to hit him with her ladle. Then more hands took hold of him from all sides and he was hoisted into the air onto a pair of shoulders. Willie hung on to someone's ear with one hand and to his sign with the other. The lunchroom was a sea of moving faces, laughing and shouting up at him. The rest of O Group was being carried too. A swarm of kids shared Henry, and Amanda's arms were wrapped in a stranglehold around the necks of two seventh-graders. She'd lost her sign. Willie saw it bob up out of the crowd. It was being passed from hand to hand.

He spotted Mrs. Cleft standing by the trash cans.

As he was carried past, Willie saw her slam her ladle down on top of a pile of dirty trays, untie her apron, wad it up, and throw it on the floor. He tried to keep her in sight, but he lost his balance and almost pitched over backward. When he looked again, she was gone.

Riding on people's shoulders was bumpy and uncomfortable, but Willie didn't care if it went on forever. I'm pretty high up, he thought, about as high as anyone can get. This is what it must be like to be as tall as a center in the big league. He wondered if he could touch the ceiling. Not quite, he decided, but if he were in the gym and had a basketball instead of a sign there was no doubt in his mind that he could stuff it, without even touching the hoop. Easy.

13

TWO... THREE... FOUR... Willie held the telephone to his ear and counted the rings. He was just about to hang up and try later when the ringing stopped.

"Hello, hello, hello. . ."

"Hi. Is Thelma there?" asked Willie.

"Yes."

Willie waited. Nothing seemed to be happening at the other end. He thought he could hear breathing.

"Hello?" he said again.

"Hello, hello, hello. This is Thelma's brother."

"Look. Can I speak to her, please? Tell her it's Willie."

"Okay, but you didn't ask me that in the beginning." The receiver clunked.

It seemed ages before Thelma picked up. "Hi, Willie. Sorry I took so long, but I was right in the middle of my turn and guess what? I'm playing Scrabble with my mother and I just zapped her. I made *garrote*—double letter score for the *G* ... fifty-point bonus for using all seven letters. She's still adding up all my points. She's going to owe me a mint. What are you calling for? I gotta get back to find out how much I made."

"I just wanted to tell you I'm not going—I'm not going to move to E Group tomorrow." When Thelma didn't say anything, he went on, a little faster. "I've been thinking about it all weekend. I don't know anyone in E Group that well. And besides, O Group isn't so bad. I'm going to see Dillworth first thing in the morning or as soon as I can. That's all. You can go back to your Scrabble." There was a long silence. Willie wondered if she was still there.

"Right," said Thelma finally. "I'll stick too, and we can go to Dillworth together. Okay?"

"Okay."

"Good. See you tomorrow."

That wasn't so hard, thought Willie.

Now Amanda. Maybe it was too late to call. He looked at the clock. Nobody went to bed at five minutes to eight. When the big hand reaches the twelve, I'll start dialing, he decided.

"Oh, Willie," said Amanda when she came to the phone. "Perfect timing. It's a commercial. I can talk. Zelly and I are watching *National Velvet.* I'm going to do a book report on it as soon as I find out how it ends. We'll probably have to do a lot of them now that we're E's."

"I'll make it quick," said Willie. "I just wanted to tell you I'm not going—I'm not going to move to E Group tomorrow."

"What!" shrieked Amanda. Willie held the phone away from his ear. "What do you mean not going? Nobody doesn't not go when they're promoted. Absolutely nobody!"

"Well, I'm not and neither is Thelma," said Willie. "We're going to see Dillworth in the morning."

"Oh, blither," Amanda wailed, "my program is on again. I have to get off this phone. I'm missing a good part. But I'll tell you one thing that I know for sure," she added before she hung up. "Mrs. Dillworth is going to think you've lost your marbles."

• •

"Can I have heard you correctly?" Mrs. Dillworth put a hand to her forehead and closed her eyes. "Some days I feel as if I'm losing my mind."

"Amanda's still going," said Willie, "if that helps."

"Who said?" Amanda put her hands on her hips and scowled at Willie. "I wouldn't dream of going. Grace would be lost without me."

Mrs. Dillworth opened her eyes and gazed at her pink lampshade. She picked up a pencil and began to roll it between her fingers. The only sound was the steady hum of the ventilator. "I wonder if you've thought this through carefully," she said at last to the air above their heads. "Have you considered the best way to fulfill your potential? Do you think this decision will expand your horizons? And allow enough room for intellectual growth? In short, are you sure you have put the saddle on the right horse?"

"Yes," said Willie. "We've thought of all that. We can do it in O Group."

"I must say you do seem to work well together," said Mrs. Dillworth after a pause. "Your performance in the lunchroom made that perfectly clear. Highly imaginative. Most creative. I liked your initiative."

"Then we can stay where we are?" asked Thelma.

"Far be it from me to stand in your way," said Mrs. Dillworth. "You seem to know exactly what you want"—she pointed at them with her pencil—"and, I might add, exactly how to get it. I do admire people who paddle their own canoes."

"There's just one other thing," said Willie. "All of us need to use the big shelves in the library."

Mrs. Dillworth's mouth twitched. "The big shelves? All of you?" She wagged her pencil in the air. "I think that can be arranged. Francis will need help and guidance, of course, but the librarian and I can work together hand in glove, so to speak. By the way, that reminds me: Do you happen to remember the thesaurus? It's still missing and it's a matter of the highest priority. You can't imagine how lost we are without it."

"Oh, we can. We can," said Amanda.

"Do keep your eyes peeled for it then," Mrs. Dillworth said. "The librarian would be more than grateful to the person or persons who return it."

"We'll sniff around," said Thelma.

"I think I may have a tiny, tiny clue already," said Amanda.

"You always say that, Amanda," said Willie hurriedly. "She says that about everything, Mrs. Dillworth, but we'll all start looking."

"That's that then," said Mrs. Dillworth, rising. She looked at her watch. "Isn't this your lunch period?"

"Usually," said Willie, "but we're skipping it."

"But it's pizza. Don't you children all love pizza?"

"Pizza!" said Thelma. "Mrs. Cleft *never* serves pizza.

"Mrs. Cleft is gone. She asked for a leave of absence, I believe. An unexpected illness in her family—very sudden. She had to take the bus Friday night."

It's too good to be true, thought Willie. "I'll believe it when I see it," he said.

"Which? Cleft or pizza?" asked Thelma under her breath.

"Both."

There was no menu taped to the wall of the cafeteria and no Mrs. Cleft anywhere, but the smell of hot cheese and tomato sauce was unmistakably pizza. And in the lunchroom there were pizzas—or what was left of them—on round tinfoil platters in the center of each table.

"Guess who's gone!" Grace announced to Willie as he pulled out his chair. "Mrs. Cleft!"

"We know," said Amanda.

"And everyone's been congratulating us," added Jonathan.

"They have?" Amanda smoothed her hair and smiled at the lunchroom before she sat down.

Henry explained about the pizza.

"There's plain or meatball, both with double cheese. You get two pieces, but it's a hard choice. Either you can have one of each or two of the same kind. And you can make your own salads at the cafeteria counter."

"Thanks for leaving us some," said Willie, reaching toward the closest platter with both hands, "but there's one here with the end bitten off."

"It used to be mine," said Henry. "I only had a slice and a bite. You can finish it if you want. I'm having seconds on salad and fruit instead."

"It's even good lukewarm," Willie said, reeling a long string of mozzarella cheese around his tongue. He chewed and swallowed. "Guess what, you guys!" he said before he took another bite. "We ran into Dillworth and she's going to arrange it so we can all use the big shelves. We can read anything we want from now on. Expand our horizons and stuff."

"Boy! First pizza, then the big shelves," said Henry.

"We seem to be winning on all fronts," said Jonathan.

"But we've got to return the thesaurus," Amanda told them. "Mrs. Dillworth asked us again to look for it and it's only fair."

"Yeah. She's right. We do," agreed Willie.

"It's not such a bad deal," said Thelma. "She gets the thesaurus; we get the big shelves."

"Still, I wish we could have both," said Beegee.

"Wait a minute!" Amanda shot forward in her chair as though she had been stuck with a pin. "Wait a little minute. I have a birthday coming up." She smiled around the table. "Aaand, I've just mailed the invitations to my party." She smiled again at each one of them this time. "Aaand, you know what you have at birthday parties, don't you? Favors!" She sang it out. "Hint, hint." She elbowed Beegee in the ribs.

"I hope boys are invited too," said Fuzzle.

Amanda just rolled her eyes and hummed a few bars of "Happy Birthday."

"Maybe I'll have them bound in leather," she said.

"Who gets to take the library copy back? There's a reward, remember? Or at least there used to be," said Grace.

"Draw straws," said Thelma, "with pieces of napkin. Here. Hand me that one. I'll rip it up."

Fuzzle drew the shortest piece and they all went with him to get the book out of Willie's locker. That was the last they saw of him until dismissal. He turned up again then, waiting by Willie's locker, as if he'd been there all the time. When he caught sight of them through the mob of kids, he beckoned wildly.

"I've got something to tell you," he said as soon as Willie was close enough to hear. "Actually, I guess I'll have to show you. It's too hard to explain."

"First," said Thelma, "did you get rid of the thesaurus?"

"And what did she say?" asked Jonathan.

"Who?" asked Fuzzle.

"The librarian. What did she say when you gave it back?" repeated Grace.

"Oh," said Fuzzle. "The librarian? I didn't exactly see the librarian."

"What do you mean, not exactly?" Willie's shoulders hunched forward.

"I couldn't find her," said Fuzzle. "I looked everywhere. That's why I went to the auditorium, in case there was a Book Fair or something. But they were just straightening up. The custodian—"

"We don't care about the custodian—" interrupted Willie. "What did you do with the book?"
"I gave it to the nurse," said Fuzzle.
To the nurse, thought Willie. What'll we do now? He wondered if he ought to go after it. Then he decided it was all right. The nurse was no ninny. She'd know what to do with it.
"But that's not the point," Fuzzle was saying. "I found something. A great new place for us to meet."
"I'm absolutely positively not going into any gross cleaning closet again," said Amanda.
"It's not a closet," said Fuzzle.
"A room. A real room?" asked Henry.
"Yes. And it's big, really big."
"Does it smell? That's all I care about," said Grace.
"Well, no. I mean I didn't notice any."
"Isn't someone using it?" asked Jonathan.
"No. It's only got some stuff in it. Like tables."
"A table could be useful," said Jonathan.
"And chairs. Lots of chairs," Fuzzle added.
"Fuzz, you're a genius!" said Willie.
"It's fantastic!" exclaimed Grace. "A huge room with tables and chairs, that no one ever uses."
"Well, uh. It's not exactly ... I mean, you make it sound. . ." Fuzzle's voice trailed away.
"No kidding, Fuzz. You're a whiz," said Thelma. "Show it to us."
Fuzzle led the way to the third floor and into the auditorium. He marched down the center aisle between the rows of empty seats, almost as if he were still in the lunchroom carrying his sign, and stopped in front of the raised stage. Stairs ran up to the stage on each side, but Fuzzle ignored them. Instead, he took hold of a brass ring set into the low wall in front of him and tugged. A long panel slid back revealing an opening about three feet high.

"You're kidding!" said Thelma. "Under the stage? You've got to be kidding."

"No, I'm not. Just wait," said Fuzzle. He dropped to all fours and crawled through the hole. When he was quite far in, he sat down cross-legged and grinned back at them. "Great, huh?"

"Awful," said Amanda. "You'll never get me in there. It's for dwarfs. I'll be a hunchback. Ruin my posture."

All Willie could see really clearly was the white of Fuzzle's teeth.

"I think I smell something already," sniffed Grace.

"I think I *hear* something—something scratching," said Henry.

"It's just Fuzzle. Get in," said Willie. "At least give it a try."

They crept in, one after another. Amanda waited until last, hesitated, and then followed, walking on her fingers and toes to keep her skirt and knees off the floor.

"Close the door after you," Willie told her. Amanda slid the panel half shut, using the palms of her hands. O Group sat in the semidarkness surrounded by the black stacks of extra chairs and folding tables that the school custodian stored there for special events.

Even so, there was plenty of room, just as Fuzzle had said. I imagined it wrong, thought Willie. Actually it was even better than Fuzzle had said.

"The only trouble is, we can't see," said Thelma after a while.

"Flashlights. We need flashlights," suggested Beegee.

"No problem," said Amanda. She sounded almost cheerful. "I'll have to have two favors instead of one at my party. That's all. Zelly will love it."

"I just thought of something awful," said Henry. "Supposing they turn this place into an office too?"

"It would be just our rotten luck," said Grace.

"I don't think our luck's so terrible," said Beegee. "We're lucky Fuzzle found this place. No one would think of using it but us."

"I think our luck's super!" said Thelma.

"It was more than luck," Willie said. He looked around at the circle of shadowy figures. Actually, it wasn't luck at all, he decided. "It was us."